Larry,

It's a joey working with
you at Post 7.

May you read this
in good health & spirits!

Your Friend,

Jason

THE RED BOX

NOVEL ANTI-GRAVITY DEVICE THAT CHANGES AMERICA

JASON O'NEIL

authorHOUSE®

AuthorHouse™
1663 Liberty Drive
Bloomington, IN 47403
www.authorhouse.com
Phone: 1 (800) 839-8640

This is a novel, and although it contains actual businesses and locations, this is a work of fiction and incorporates fictional elements and events. Any similarity between the characters in this book and actual persons is purely coincidental and unintentional. The book is primarily about the development of a new type of aircraft. The Boeing Company and Mercedes-Benz are both highlighted in this fiction due to their global transportation prowess and expertise. Nothing in the book is intended to convey or imply facts about any persons or products of these businesses.

Character descriptions can be found in the appendix.

Published by AuthorHouse 04/28/2015

ISBN: 978-1-5049-0934-1 (sc)
ISBN: 978-1-5049-0935-8 (e)

Library of Congress Control Number: 2015906721

Print information available on the last page.

This book is printed on acid-free paper.

Contents

Chapter 1

BALDIE

Just as Matt was putting his cell phone down on the table, he looked up to see a white speck on the blue sky's horizon to the north of the Sunbreeze Hotel on Ambergris Caye in Belize. He looked down at his Patek Philippe wristwatch and said, "Right on time. Let's go down to the pier and invite the crew for a drink and tell them the good news."

The white speck continued to grow in size as it approached. Within a couple of minutes, the outline of an aircraft could be discerned. There was no noise. It just glided slowly down to the water.

The Flynn brothers, Matt and Murray, both smiled with a quiet delight. No words were spoken as they walked down to the pier.

Coming down to about 200 feet, the aircraft resembled a small version of the Space Shuttle. It was white and had four porthole windows on each side. As the craft banked slightly, the late afternoon sun illuminated the large bald eagle logo on the tail. Each brother thought to himself, "What a magnificent bird!"

The tourists who were standing in the beach surge couldn't take their eyes off the unique craft. They watched with real excitement as the aircraft splashed down about 200 yards off the end of the pier. The brothers walked out to the end of the pier followed by two bronzed honeymooners. As the craft, now a seaplane, approached the pier at about 6 knots, Matt and Murray each picked up a line for the tie-down.

The almost disbelieving new husband asked, "What is *that*?"

Matt replied, "It's a Baldie." The couple looked at each other and shrugged their shoulders. "What do you mean, sir?" the man asked.

Matt replied, "It's a new form of transportation between the Belize mainland and the islands like Ambergris Caye. It's quite safe because it's both an airplane and a seaplane."

"Can we look inside? Maybe get a ride someday? I'm a private pilot and would really enjoy the experience," the honeymooner said.

"Maybe someday," Murray said. "It's only a prototype undergoing tests."

The honeymooners sat on a bench as the brothers tied off Baldie. They could see the pilot give the thumbs-up gesture from the cockpit.

A minute later the hatch opened and a gangplank slid out to the pier. A male and female pilot strode quickly down the gangplank. A third person soon appeared in the hatch. The male pilot, a tall, handsome man with the demeanor of a Navy commodore, called out, "Aaron, shut him down for the night and bring the test laptop and Red Box to me at the veranda."

"Will do, Captain," he said with a small salute. The female pilot, a tall, slender figure with Asian features, walked over to Murray and gave him a peck on the cheek. He put his arm around his wife and nodded approvingly.

Matt asked the Captain, "Jim, is everything according to spec?"

The pilot responded, "Yes, AOK. I'll show you the data in the laptop."

"Fine. And we've got something important to tell you. Wait until you hear this!"

"Let's head into the veranda. José has a little concoction he wants us to try," Matt said. "And, seeing as we're now off-duty, an adult beverage is in order."

They all chuckled.

The pilots picked up their flight cases and the party of four headed into shore. About halfway down the pier, Murray turned around. He could see the male honeymooner intently inspecting the Baldie.

Ten minutes later the pilots had changed into their Tommy Bahama outfits and joined Matt and Murray at a table away from the bar in a secluded alcove ringed by orange hibiscus. They used this table so much, they often referred to it as their "Stammtisch," like a reserved table in a German bier stube.

A fifth person walked up to the table carrying a black ballistic fabric satchel. He was the Baldie co-pilot, Aaron Adams, who bore a striking resemblance to Matt Damon.

"Captain, here's what you asked for," Aaron said as he set the satchel down on the flagstone next to Jim Russell's chair. He took a seat across the table next to Maggie.

The captain reached down into the satchel and pulled out a laptop and powered it on. With Matt and Murray at his side, he watched as the display lit up with myriad colored charts. Captain Russell pointed to several of the squiggly lines and the brothers nodded approvingly.

Matt asked, "How was the vertical takeoff?" Captain Russell responded, "Here's the power profile. It was flawless and, indeed, much faster than the previous ones."

"I knew it!" Murray said.

Matt said, "The Red Box is outperforming our estimates." He looked around the table and asked, "Any questions?" Silence was consent.

The captain was putting away the laptop when José Flores, the debonair resort manager, approached the table with a tray of cocktail glasses.

"I hope you had a good day, my friends," he said as he warmly greeted the team.

"So what's the surprise, José?" asked Matt.

José set the tray down on the table and distributed the cocktails around the table.

"Well, in honor of your wonderful patronage here at the Sunbreeze these past months, I have invented a new drink. The team slowly raised their glasses and clinked them. They examined the beverage's yellow-orange hue and took a drink as José said, "Salut, my friends."

After a few seconds, Maggie asked, "What is it? It's fabulous. It feels so healthy!"

José quickly responded, "It's two parts Orangina and one part rum with a wedge of lime."

With pride in his voice, José announced, "It's a Baldie."

The table erupted in joyous laughter.

"I trust it's emblematic of a real winner!" José said.

Another round of laughter followed.

Aaron said, "This is terrific. I could really get used to these ... even for breakfast!"

Another round of laughter erupted.

Matt addressed José. "My friend, your hospitality is again overwhelming. Yes, this could be the team's drink of choice."

José smiled like a happy innkeeper who had pleased his guests, bowed slightly, and returned to the veranda bar. He called back to the group, "Let me know if you want another round. It's on the house."

Captain Russell then asked, "What's this good news you mentioned down on the pier?"

Murray looked intently at the surrounding foliage as if to detect any listening devices. Maggie knew what he was thinking.

In a very low tone, almost whispering, Matt said, "We've got our patents. The paper documents arrived by FedEx, and we just got off the phone with John Baldinger."

"Terrific!" exclaimed Aaron. Maggie's face lit up with joy.

Matt continued, "The Red Box is unencumbered by other claims. We have both design and process patents. There is nothing else like it on Earth. We are cleared to increase production of the current design. Just think — we committed to this technology over two years ago. Now we're rewarded with U.S. patents, and soon I hope our checkbook will also be rewarded."

"That's great," Captain Russell said. "What happens now?"

Matt looked around the table, making eye contact with each team member. "Murray and Maggie will return to Miami to start with second production line and check the progress of our backup, second site," he said. "I will join you in a couple of weeks. I will also alert Paula Frankel at the Federal Aviation Administration about the patent and the need for silence about our program. Maybe I'm paranoid, but I can't help feel that somebody's watching us, even here in Belize. I will also confirm the schedule when we can brief the commissioner and his team. And I have half a mind to invite Ms. Frankel to Belize to personally participate in the flight tests."

Matt paused, looked around the table again at his rapt audience, and continued. "So, Jim, this means you and Aaron will need to accelerate the test program. I want to beat the rainy season, which starts in June.

And I want more data and videos to show investors and the FAA for the flight safety certificate. Armed with the patents, the sales job should be a lot easier."

"We can do it," the captain replied.

"Good. I thought so," Matt said. "Please convene the team here for breakfast so we can devise a plan."

"Will do, sir," the captain replied.

Matt continued, "What do you say? I think a quiet dinner celebration is in order."

All faces smiled and heads nodded approvingly.

Matt ended the meeting by saying, "You know, I just might have another Baldie in honor of the occasion."

He turned around to see José at the bar, then raised his hand and spread out five fingers.

José smiled.

Chapter 2

WEIGHTLESS

The next morning Murray and Maggie took the water taxi from San Pedro to Belize City on the mainland. Early in the afternoon they boarded a commercial jet to Miami. As they deplaned at Miami International Airport, Maggie interrupted Murray, who was deep in thought.

"Murray," she said, "I've enjoyed helping with the Baldie test program. However, one thing's missing."

"What's that?" her husband asked with a quizzical look on his face.

"How does the Red Box work?" she asked rather assertively.

"Honey, as you know, for safety and security purposes, only Matt and I know its real secrets."

"Yes, I know that and understand why," she said. "But I want to help increase the production, so I thought I should know more about this miracle technology that you've invented."

Murray was flattered and responded, "Yes, you're right. I can explain a little more about it and walk you through the process tomorrow morning at the production facility."

"Perfect," said Maggie, who carried a small smile on her face all the way from the airport to their home on Key Biscayne.

Early the next morning, the couple drove southwest down Route 1, the Dixie Highway, to 72ⁿᵈ Street and turned south two blocks to a gated facility. As they entered the building, they were greeted by the assistant factory manager, Don Carlos Fuentes, a ruggedly good-looking man with a broad smile.

"Welcome, Maggie," he said. "We certainly can use your help in our expansion program."

Maggie responded, "Thank you, Don Carlos. I look forward to it very much, and maybe I'll get to see more of my husband in the process."

The three of them laughed as Murray led them to Maggie's new office, a small room just outside Test Room #1. Don Carlos excused himself and entered a glass-enclosed room that reminded Maggie of a biotechnology lab she took while in college.

Murray and Maggie then entered an airflow passageway where they put on smocks and gauze head covers. They stepped on an airwash mat and entered the test room. Murray opened a large safe and pulled out a bright red box about the size of a military ammunition box and placed it in the center of a workbench.

"Well, here it is, Maggie. This is what all the excitement is about," he said.

Maggie warned her husband, "OK, my dear. But you're the mad scientist–genius physicist. Please keep the explanation in layman's seven-word sentences."

"I'll try my best," said Murray, who at that moment looked like another, slightly better known physicist: J. Robert Oppenheimer.

"You know that everything is made of molecules. Molecules are composed of atomic particles — protons, neutrons, and electrons. In simple terms, the key is to harness the energy expended by electrons as they whirl around the nucleus. The Red Box, when activated on a host carrier, like a Baldie, absorbs these electrons, or a portion thereof. This energy is trapped in the Red Box, which neutralizes the downward pull of gravity on the host platform. The result is a neutral buoyancy field which surrounds the object. The object becomes weightless and can then be propelled upward and/or forward with an extremely small propulsion system relative to the size of the host platform."

"It seems too simple to work," Maggie said.

"That may be, my dear," Murray said. "But you've flown in a Baldie and experienced it for yourself."

"Yes, I have," Maggie said. "And I particularly enjoy when Baldie goes straight up like the flying saucers in sci-fi movies."

Murray continued, "There are no complex electrical circuits to overcharge or burn out. There are only a couple of wires leading to the power-on LED test port and standard power receptacle for a trickle charge from the host platform. The Red Box has a small battery for a four-hour reserve, sufficient to fly almost anywhere. And external energy sources such as leaking power towers, lightning bolts, and even solar flares do not affect the energy field. The simplicity of the Red Box is an important part of the patent protection.

"And the patents are sufficiently broad, yet vague, such that the Red Box cannot be easily duplicated or reverse-engineered. The box is sealed to prevent tampering, much less disablement. It becomes useless if opened by unauthorized parties.

"There are only eight components which compose a Red Box. We buy seven of the components and assemble them here. The eighth component is the Electron Absorption Media, or EAM, which is manufactured in the next room and inserted in the Red Box," he said as he pointed through the window to the clean assembly room. "The LED lights up when the EAM is fully saturated and ready for operation."

Murray put his hand on the Red Box and picked it up by the handle and said, "The handle is a GPS system antenna for tracking its location when it is outside a host platform or vehicle."

He continued, "We don't want Baldie falling from the sky. After all, you might be on board, my love. Therefore, testing in this room is a critical part of the production process — precisely where you can help once you are trained."

He picked up two pieces of metal. "You see these end brackets? They are used to mount and secure the Red Box during vibration, temperature, and spurious microwave energy testing. Then the Red Box, called an 'RB' around here, is placed in a special fixture and activated to verify its anti-gravity properties."

Murray motioned to Maggie to come over to a window between Test Room #1 and Test Room #2. She saw a young woman in a pilot's suit and helmet floating around the room in a one-person capsule tethered to a bank of computers and displays.

"Wow! Can I do that?" Maggie asked.

Murray responded with a cautious tone, "Well, maybe someday … if you're good." He continued, "Test failures are unacceptable. If they occur, the Red Box is immediately destroyed and recycled."

"And I hope you understand, I can't show you the EAM production process. Even though it's now patented, it's proprietary to Matt and me for security purposes. We are the only two people who know what's in it and how it functions in a Red Box. And, as you know, that's why my brother and I never travel together on the same mode of transportation."

"Yes, I've noticed," Maggie said.

Murray further explained, "All of the assemblers are thoroughly screened to the Top Secret level, bonded, and must undergo an annual polygraph test to ensure integrity and absolute secrecy. As Matt indicated to you, we have cloned this facility at a classified location on a closed military base on a different power grid. And, of course, vendors and suppliers drop ship their items at a third-party location so they never see the production process."

"So, honey, there you have it!" Murray said with some pride in his voice. "The box and the process are simple, enabling a quick increase in production once the employees are screened and the facility is ready, complete with the appropriate security systems and procedures in place. Any questions?"

"Yes. What about the Baldie? Where is he made?"

"You know I've come home late many evenings over these past two years," Murray replied. I've been in Homestead, Florida. The Baldie is manufactured in a special hangar 12 miles southwest of here at the Homestead General Aviation Airport. It's on 217th Avenue adjacent to Everglades National Park. It's remote for security purposes. But this little airport has an Executive Jet Center, so we have a good pool of employees from which to draw. The first five Baldies will be made there until a major production facility can be found elsewhere in America. The initial test flights are made at night out over the Everglades.

"When the initial checkouts are complete, the Baldie flies south over the Gulf of Mexico to Belize for final flight certification tests where you assisted as a technician.

"That's the whole story, my dear," Murray said as he put the Red Box back into the safe.

"Well, it seems that you Flynn brothers have thought of everything," Maggie said. "What's next?"

"To make money!" Murray eagerly answered.

"Oh, I get it," Maggie responded. "You plan to use a couple of Baldies to ferry tourists between Caribbean and Central American locations, and it's safe because it's also a seaplane."

"Yes," Murray said. "That's the initial application because we thought it would be the easiest to flight-certify with the FAA. But it's only the beginning!"

"What do you mean?" Maggie asked.

"The use of a Red Box by a government or corporate entity is negotiated on a case-by-case basis via license agreement with a large, possibly $1 billion usage fee for a limited period, subject to renewal restrictions and additional fees. Also, advertising and endorsement contracts are granted via auction and limited in markets and license periods.

"Matt is keen to have the Red Box be part of Government-funded national transportation infrastructure projects at the national and state levels, which are eligible for long-term fee payment plans. And you know our politics: anti-democratic governments and entities need not apply."

"And you really feel this is all possible?" Maggie asked.

"I do indeed, my dear. We'll prove that the Red Box is the largest job creator in human history. But let's save that topic for another day. Right now we're due to meet with our production manager, José Diaz, to discuss the expansion program."

Maggie glanced at the safe as they left Test Room #1 and thought to herself, "Murray never exaggerated in his life."

Chapter 3

PARADISE

One week later the patent attorney, John Baldinger, arrived at the Sunbreeze to discuss patents relative to the Baldie and presentations in forthcoming investor meetings.

Matt Flynn held out his hand and warmly shook Baldinger's hand as he said, "Welcome to our little paradise, John." Baldinger, who resembled Liam Neeson with a mustache and horn-rimmed reading glasses, was quick to say, "Are you kidding me? I'm so glad to get out of Washington, D.C., and see you and Baldie in person. You know, when I first heard the name 'Baldie,' I thought you had named the craft after me. That was my nickname in college."

Matt replied, "No such luck. It's named for the bald eagle, the top of the bird food chain." They both laughed. "Of course, the bald eagle survived near extinction in America, but our Baldie won't be faced with that predicament. The flights tests have been amazing and exceeding all of the specifications."

"That's good to hear," Baldinger said.

"You'll get a firsthand tour in the morning and see the Red Box in action," Matt said as he put his arm around his friend. "Let's meet here in the lobby at 7. Dinner's on me, and I'll give you the background you need to complete our Baldie design patent."

The two friends met at 7. Matt promptly escorted John to the veranda bar, where they took a table under several palm trees.

"So, Matt, I have to ask you a burning question," Baldinger said.

"Oh?"

"Yes. Why Belize? It's gorgeous, but why here?"

"John, I did my homework, and this place is a winner in all categories. It's the only Central American country settled by the English, and therefore, the national language is English. English law prevails. Plus, it's only two hours from Miami and Houston. The first Baldie tests are over water for safety, and he's a seaplane, so we test in local lagoons and on the Gulf."

Matt pointed west as he explained, "Baldie takes off and lands at airports, and there's an airport only four blocks from here.

"Another criteria is climate. The weather here is perfect, particularly between January and May, when the rains are infrequent. And there are no hurricanes.

"Needless to say, the pilots and test engineers love it here. In addition to several five-star restaurants here in San Pedro, there are a thousand Mayan ruins to explore. And look out there, John," Matt said as he pointed eastward. "There's a great barrier reef for some of the world's best snorkeling with an average water temperature of 80 degrees.

"And my bank, the Caye International Bank, is just four blocks from here. It has an agreement with the United States to prevent money-laundering, along with excellent relations with Swiss banks."

"I'm getting the picture, Matt," John said. "Indeed, I'm starting to really like this place myself." He put his arms above his head and took in a deep breath of the warm seashore breeze.

"Now let me introduce you to a Baldie," Matt said.

"What do you mean?" John asked.

"You'll see what I mean in a couple minutes." On cue José brought over two tumblers with an orange-colored cocktail.

John clinked his glass with Matt, then took a sip and said, "Wow! This is really good! Don't tell me it's a health drink."

"Well, not exactly," Matt said. "It has Orangina, but it's also a good use of rum."

A few minutes later, Matt led John on a walk downtown to one of his favorite restaurants, a French bistro, where they enjoyed each other's company the rest of the evening.

The next morning Matt and John finished their breakfast of coffee, fresh fruit in a conch shell, and Mayan cornmeal pancakes.

"Do you suppose the Mayans ate these pancakes thousands of years ago?" John asked.

"I don't know, but they're pretty darn good!" Matt replied.

A few minutes later Matt took his barrister friend on the four-block walk to the airport.

They walked up to Hangar 26 and were about to enter a side door when John asked, "What's with the number 26? There are only three buildings here."

"Yes, I know," Matt said. "It's the airport director's favorite number. It works for me."

"Fair enough," John replied.

Just as they walked in the door, the hangar door rolled to the side, allowing the bright morning sun to illuminate the white craft.

They walked slowly around the one-of-a-kind plane, and John turned on a small tape recorder as Matt described the Baldie.

"It's about one-fifth the size of the Space Shuttle, with engines that allow travel on the water or in the air.

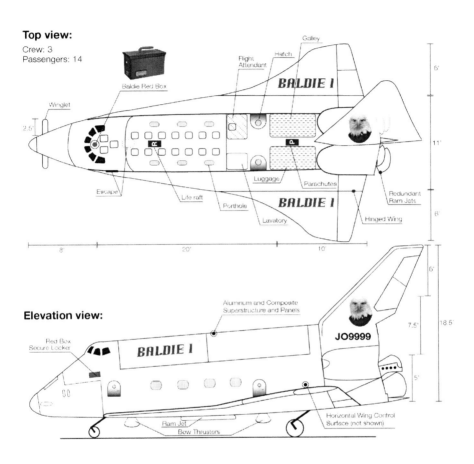

Top view:

Crew: 3
Passengers: 14

Elevation view:

Key BRB Specifications

Length: 38' Beam: 23' with horizontal wing deployed
Beam: 11' for marina slip launch

Draft: 5'

Passengers: 14; Crew: 3

Weight: 22 Tons – Wet   Luggage: 2000 lbs.

Speed: 350/210 mph (maximum/cruise)

Range/Distance: 1,200 miles   Fuel: 350 gal.

Power: 2 Kamewa Waterjets, convertible for Ramjet Airborne flight, bow thrusters

Figure 1.1: Caribbean Tourist Configuration

"It's sized to carry 14 passengers and a crew of three principally as a shuttle between the mainland and the islands and among the islands, ideally in the Gulf and Caribbean.

"And it's sized to be scalable, either larger or smaller, even personal size like a three-person Ski-Doo.

"The Red Box makes it weightless so it can rise straight up like a helicopter. And because it's weightless, only small, fuel-efficient engines are needed for propulsion."

John interrupted Matt.

"And the logo. The bald eagle is much nicer than my picture would be." They both laughed.

"It weighs about 22 tons with full fuel," Matt continued. "But you would never know it. Captain Russell reports that it responds to feather-touch handling. And with only a 5-foot draft and slight activation of the Red Box, it literally flies over the water. It makes the water taxi that brought you over here from Belize City seem like a horse and buggy.

"The superstructure is aluminum with composite panels to reduce weight and maintenance, much like the Boeing Dreamliner."

John said, "You've given me a dozen patent claims already. What in your mind are some of the others?"

"Well, I thought you'd ask," Matt said as he handed his friend a piece of paper. On it was a list of potential claims:

- Three-in-one craft application of the Red Box airplane, seaplane, and helicopter
- Two Kamewa waterjets converted for ramjet airborne flight
- Combination of waterjet and dual bow thrusters to enable the vertical ascent
- Snap-on engine module for quick repair to maximize service time

- Five-foot draft enables powerboat that quickly exceed 45 knots (and of course it can fly above any sea state)
- Hinged wings that fold up to enable use in standard marine slips
- Secure Red Box, lockable receptor bracket with quick change-out in flight if necessary
- Dual parachutes to enable low-rate horizontal splashdown if necessary
- Nose winglets for high-speed stability and control
- Modular seat platform which can be swapped out for a cargo or patient litter module in less than 15 minutes
- Large windows for tourists to view the scenery

"If that isn't enough, John, here's a memory stick with a complete set of drawings, parts list, and specifications," Matt said as he handed a flash drive to John. "There are only three of these. One's locked in a safe in Miami and one is for use by the FAA flight certification team here in Belize. I trust you with it. It must always be on your person or in a safe."

John nodded his understanding. He knew just how serious Matt was about security around the Red Box and the Baldie.

As they were ending their walk-around, Captain Russell approached them. Matt introduced him and the captain asked John, "Well, what do you think of our proud bird?"

"It's incredible, simply incredible," John replied.

"Are you able to be a passenger to witness some of our tests this afternoon?" Captain Russell asked.

"I sure am, Captain!"

"Great. It should be fun. We're going to do a series of touch-and-gos on the back bay. You'll get a firsthand experience of how capable our eagle really is. Please be back here by 2 p.m."

"Yes, sir!"

After lunch, the eager lawyer returned to the airport with his Nikon in hand. Baldie was already over at the access ramp, floating next to the pier. Members of the technical crew were at their stations. John clicked his seatbelt and gave a thumbs-up sign to co-pilot Adams. Only one minute later Baldie was skimming across the bay. Matt, who came down to watch the launch, pictured the broad smile on his friend's face.

That evening some of the crew joined Matt and John for dinner on the beach, Hawaiian style. They relived the day's flight. John proudly showed them some of the pictures he took.

As they relaxed over dessert Matt said, "John, my friend, I think you've gained in-depth knowledge about our craft. But there's one more thing I would like you to do."

"What's that?"

"Go home via Miami. I have arranged a detailed inspection of Baldie 2 at Homestead. I'm sure you'll uncover another dozen claims. Maggie's ready to be your tour guide."

"Matt, plan on it. You know me — I'll be a Sherlock Holmes on the case."

"Thanks. I knew I could count on you, John. And, by the way, the goal for the Baldie application is one month from today. OK?"

"OK."

The next morning, John said goodbye to the test team and hopped a golf cart to the water taxi terminal for the 20-minute trip to Belize City. Matt caught up with him via cell phone and said, "John, I may ask you to defend our claims before a group of investors in Alabama next month. Please be ready. Bon voyage."

Chapter 4

NINJA

Red Box Production Facility #1 occupies a former Elks Lodge on Southwest 78th Street two blocks from Route 1 in South Miami. It is a gated compound with a 20,000-square-foot building with offices, a clean room assembly area, two test rooms, loading docks, a break room, picnic area, and parking lot for 30 cars. The Flynns spent a year and a million dollars refurbishing the building to meet their needs.

The glass-enclosed clean room resembles a biotechnology laboratory. The site's two dozen employees wear smocks and hair caps. Offices are set up for Matt, Murray, José, Maggie, and a visitor like a U.S. Government inspector. The test rooms include temperature chambers, vibration tables, monitoring racks, and a safe for overnight storage.

On a cool night in February, José and Maggie were working late. José was in his office, catching up on paperwork, and Maggie was running a noisy vibration test of a Red Box. Around 11 p.m. two masked ninja figures climbed over the picnic area wall in the back of the building, picked the lock of a door, and immediately disarmed the security sensor and cut the power at the breaker panel.

One ninja went to José's office as he was coming out to investigate the power outage. The ninja ordered him to lie facedown on the floor at gunpoint. The other ninja went to the test room and ordered Maggie to detach the Red Box from the vibration table and hand it over. The ninja then put the Red Box in a black bag, ordered Maggie to lie facedown, and ran down the hall to José's office.

Maggie crawled behind a smock locker as the thieves ran to the street-side emergency exit near Test Room #1. Maggie, a martial arts practitioner, leaped out and grabbed one of the thieves around the neck. As they scuffled, she was cut on her arm and hit on the side of her head. Dazed, she fell to the floor.

Meanwhile, José grabbed his pistol from his desk drawer and ran to the emergency exit. He fired at the dark figures, who were crawling through a hole in the fence. The thieves fired back with a hail of bullets. Maggie, still somewhat dazed, crawled to the exit door and was hit by a ricocheting bullet. A large SUV sped away into the night.

Quick to action, José returned the circuit breakers to their upright position and hurried back to help Maggie, who was bleeding profusely from a wound to her upper left chest. José grabbed a smock, put it around her chest, and tied the arms tightly to form a tight bandage.

Time was critical. So as not to dislodge the bullet, he dragged Maggie on the blood-soaked smock to the loading dock. He then backed up his SUV and gently laid her in the back. He remotely activated the facility's alarm system and sped off to South Miami Hospital, just six blocks down the Dixie Highway. As he approached the Emergency Room entrance, he skillfully avoided a car driving on the wrong side of Route 1.

As Maggie was wheeled into the hospital on a gurney, José called both Murray and Matt. "There's been a robbery tonight," he reported. "Maggie's been shot and we're at the Emergency Room at South Miami Hospital." Within 20 minutes, Matt, his wife Heather, and Murray were at the hospital.

"She's in surgery," José told the team. "If I know Maggie, she'll pull through like a champ."

Wiping his tears away, Murray cried, "I should have been there!"

José responded, "No, there was nothing you could do. And you might have been a casualty as well."

"I guess you're right," Murray moaned.

Two hours later, Dr. James Cox emerged from the operating room. With the focused, deliberate demeanor of Sean Connery, he said, "The bullet lodged an inch from her heart. She's one lucky woman. She should fully recover over time, but she's lost a lot of blood and will need plenty of rest. You can see her tomorrow morning."

The Flynns breathed a collective sigh of relief. Murray was the first to shake the doctor's hand.

At that moment, José, who had gone back to the facility to assist the police, returned to the hospital to tell his colleagues that everything was in order. Dr. Cox approached him and said, "Sir, your quick thinking was instrumental in Mrs. Flynn's survival. You stopped just enough bleeding, buying us time to get her on life support." He turned to the Flynns, put his arm around José, and said, "This man deserves a reward."

Matt said, "How about a week's vacation for you and your family in Belize?" All heads nodded approval. José smiled with pride.

The team returned to the hospital late the next morning. As they entered Maggie's room, Murray felt suddenly lightheaded. He moved a chair over to her bedside, sat down, and reached out for Maggie's hand.

Maggie managed a faint smile and said in a soft voice, "I've failed. They have a Red Box."

On the other side of the bed, Matt took her other hand, caressed it, and said, "Don't worry, Maggie. You know that the Red Box is tamper proof. The second it's opened, it is rendered useless. No formulas are divulged."

Murray's eyes met Maggie's as he nodded in agreement.

Matt added, "And we have a GPS antenna in the handle. If possible, we'll track it to the ends of the earth."

Maggie raised her bed up just as Dr. Cox entered the room.

"Mrs. Flynn, you're one lucky woman," he said as he reached for her wrist to confirm her pulse rate with the monitor. "How do you feel?"

Maggie spoke in a stronger voice, "A little weak, but buoyed by my friends and family. Thank you so much, Dr. Cox."

The doctor replied, "You're welcome, but the real gratitude should be expressed to José. His quick thinking probably saved your life."

Murray told her how they were rewarding José and his family.

"Terrific. Good idea. Thanks," Maggie said.

"Doctor, when can she come home?" Murray asked.

"She'll probably be released in a couple days, depending on her vital signs," Dr. Cox said. "But she needs total rest."

Heather was quick to speak. "She's welcome at our place to recuperate poolside with <u>no</u> work responsibilities. If we turn her over to Murray, she'll be back at work too soon!"

Everyone laughed.

Dr. Cox shook Maggie's hand and said, "I'll check on you tomorrow," before leaving the room.

The next morning, Matt called a personal friend, Chin Chin Po, a detective based in Hong Kong who was vacationing in Miami. At 5-foot-8, she was a strikingly beautiful Chinese woman with a narrow face and delicate features. She had earned a criminology degree when she graduated summa cum laude from the University of Maryland.

"Chin Chin," Matt said, "I'd like your help investigating a recent robbery at our facility. We believe the thieves are Chinese. Maggie saw a scorpion on one of the thieves' forearms. They may be based in Hong Kong."

Chin Chin responded, "Of course I'll help, Matt. And you're in luck. My associate, Tinshin Wei, is with me. She has solved several recent crimes and has earned a vacation in Miami. I trust her implicitly."

A diminutive woman, 24-year-old Tinshin was the pride of the Hong Kong Police Department for her criminology research expertise. She had a beautiful face with delicate features to match her intellect.

"We'll inquire in the small Chinatown in Miami and work leads from here," Chin Chin said. "Please be alerted: It sounds like an inside job. We'll do a background check of all of your employees since you opened the production facility."

"Thank you," Matt replied. "I knew I could count on you. The stolen Red Box is useless, but we must find out who's behind this. And my guess is he's Chinese acting on higher authority."

"I'm on it, Matt. Expect a report within a month."

"Thanks again," Matt said as he hung up the phone.

For the next 10 days, Maggie recuperated poolside at Matt Flynn's residence in Key Biscayne. Heather was a true friend, providing the emotional and physical support she needed. Murray would visit each evening to check on his sweetheart and report the progress at the plant.

One afternoon Murray caught a glimpse of her scar, only partially covered by her bikini top, as they ate a casual lunch on Matt and Heather's deck. "Wow, that was close!" he said. "Are you ready to return to Test Room #1 next week? We need you. *I* need you."

Maggie smiled and said, "Yes, I'm not cut out for the lifestyle of the rich and famous. I will be there."

Murray kissed her on the forehead and winked. "That's my girl!"

Chapter 5

FLIGHT-WORTHY

On a lovely April day a cab whisked Murray and Captain Adams from Reagan National Airport to the Mandarin Oriental Hotel in downtown Washington, D.C. As they entered the lobby, they were greeted by Matt, who had arrived on an earlier flight. About 10 minutes later, their patent attorney, John Baldinger, joined them at lunch. They rehearsed their briefing and arguments to be presented to the FAA.

At 1:30 they walked the six blocks to the FAA headquarters at 800 Independence Avenue Southwest, known as the Orville Wright building. After passing security, the team was escorted to the administrator's office, where they set up their laptop in the conference room.

At 2:15 the FAA administrator, Orin Wright, and his assistant, Paula Frankel, entered the room. The parties took seats on opposite sides of the table. Captain Russell joined via videoconference from the airport at Ambergris Caye.

Matt thanked the administrator for consenting to the meeting and quickly summarized why the Baldie team requested the briefing.

"We applied for authority to fly our new aircraft over U.S. airspace almost a year ago," Matt said. "A lot has happened since then, so we wanted to take this opportunity to bring you up to date. Our total presentation will take less than an hour. May we proceed?"

Mr. Wright nodded his approval.

Matt continued, "First I will ask my brother, Murray, to brief you about the Red Box."

Murray went to the head of the table and removed a Red Box from a ballistic cloth carrying case. He described the technology in general terms. He presented a slide show of the manufacturing process and ended his remarks by saying, "Once activated, the Red Box makes its host weightless, a fact that has gained interest at the White House and the Department of Defense. We will be briefing them shortly."

Murray then introduced John Baldinger, who took 10 minutes to summarize the patent claims. John ended his remarks by telling the hosts, "I hope you see by the breadth of the Red Box patent the hundreds if not thousands of applications for this technology and, as Matt has pointed out, the potential to create millions of jobs."

"Thank you, John," Matt said. "Sir, at this time I would like to introduce Aaron Adams, our Baldie co-pilot."

Aaron stood up and addressed the room from the head of the table, narrating a 10-minute video of Baldie 1 in flight. He then ran through a series of slides showing actual flight data statistics from the trials being conducted in Belize. Ms. Frankel, who seemed genuinely interested in the outcome of the certification process, asked several questions about the flight data.

At this point in the briefing, Matt introduced Captain Russell, who talked about the Baldie's dozens of flight safety features. "We are here in Belize because the Baldie is also a seaplane. In Belize we can maximize the testing regimens to provide your team with sufficient data to prove Baldie flight-worthy," he said. "It's an ideal locale to test the craft's ramjets and bow thrusters, which, when pointed down, enable Baldie to rise straight up to a safe altitude for transfer to horizontal flight."

"You mean, Captain, that the Baldie operates like a helicopter as well?" Mr. Wright asked.

"Yes, sir," responded Captain Russell, who answered several more questions before signing off on his videoconference.

Matt ended the meeting with a statement about the national importance of the project for economic, social, and potentially military reasons. He requested that the certification be given a sense of urgency and be performed at the highest security level. He then thanked the FAA representatives for their time.

Mr. Wright spoke: "Gentlemen, you've come a long way, and while I'll admit most of what Murray said went over my head, I can plainly see the implication for global airspace. Therefore, I've appointed Paula as the deputy project manager. She will have the full support of the FAA to join the team in Belize within 10 days to bring the certification process to a successful conclusion. I hope this meets with your approval."

"Yes, sir. It sure does," Matt said. "And I will appoint Captain Adams to serve as the lead point of contact to ensure that our team is fully responsive."

Aaron's eyes lit up as his eyes met Paula's when they shook hands and said goodbye. He found himself looking forward to her arrival in Belize, and not entirely for professional reasons.

Ten days later, as the sun rose over the Gulf of Mexico, the Flynn brothers entered the Sunbreeze lobby to greet their guest. Waiting at the front desk was a strikingly beautiful brunette with piercing dark eyes and an attractive, slim physique. Her linen pantsuit seemed to flow gracefully as she approached the brothers.

"Welcome, Ms. Frankel," Matt said. "We're so glad Commissioner Wright appointed you to the team."

"Thank you, Matt. I'm really glad to get out of Washington and get some flight experience. Oh, and please call me Paula."

"Will do."

Paula turned to greet Murray, "Hello, Murray. You're so tan! I guess this place agrees with you!"

"It sure does. And the longer you're here, I think the more you'll agree."

Matt then asked their guest, "Would you kindly join us for breakfast on the veranda?"

"Sure," Paula said. "I'm eager to get the status and join the team during these final weeks."

Matt's wife, Heather, and the Baldie co-pilot, Aaron, joined the group at breakfast.

"So let me review the process so far," Matt began. "Shortly after we briefed the commissioner about a year ago, we submitted our Certification Plan and signed the requisite agreements. Four months ago your FAA team visited our Miami facilities to conduct a review of the Red Box production process. They witnessed our tests and conducted some of their own. We provided full documentation packages. I'm very pleased to report that, as you may know, last week we received the certification approval package.

"And for the past three months your FAA team has been here. The team consists of a test pilot, flight systems engineer, flight safety consultant, and an aerodynamicist computer systems modeler.

"As you'll see before this day is over, we have provided full support to your folks." Matt patted Heather on the shoulder as he continued, "Heather here has served as the primary point of contact and has compiled meeting minutes detailed like the aeronautical engineer she is.

"I'm not an expert, but our own evaluation checklists indicate that Baldie 1 is performing as predicted. And, let's face it, safety is paramount for our endeavors and the supporting investors. And should these tests prove successful and the certification be awarded, we plan to execute an initial production contract with Mercedes-Benz for the production, sales, and use of the Baldie in American airspace. But I'm doing all the talking. Do you have any questions so far?"

"Yes," Paula said. "What are the logistics of the test environment?"

"Glad you asked. As you know, Baldie is both a land-based and a water-based craft. Indeed, it's a flying boat meant to serve tourists and commuters between Caribbean locations. We're here in Belize because it's remote, but it has all of the requisite facilities to conduct both sets of tests. And heaven forbid, should there be a problem, the craft can glide to a safe water landing and power itself back here.

"We have provided two test units, Baldie 2 and Baldie 3. Baldie 1 remains in Miami as a trainer and demonstrator, and if all goes well, it will end up in the Smithsonian Air and Space Museum across the street from your office.

"This hotel is in an ideal location. It has two piers for docking, and Baldie's draft is only 6 feet. Indeed, it could come right up on the beach if it had to. And we're only four blocks from the San Pedro airport, where we have built a hangar to house the aircraft, perform maintenance, and provide offices for our team. The airport also has a pier and a landing ramp to allow Baldie easy access to the water.

"Baldie 2 has been outfitted with power racks to support your test equipment. Baldie 3 has been outfitted for commercial use, complete with seats, galley, and restroom. Complete sets of manuals and drawing packages are onboard, on the laptops, and in your offices at the hangar.

"I hope you see that we have cooperated and want this certification to be successful and on schedule. We're glad we started this six months ago with the goal of obtaining approval this summer."

Heather spoke up to detail some of the tests the team had conducted.

"We've focused on the six key test areas: manual flight; avionics and backup; instrumental flight; takeoff and landing — including induced stalls — from the runway and the water; weight and balance; and foul weather operation," she explained. "Baldie has been struck by lightning with no loss of power or control. We believe we have closed every action item to date."

"I'll second that," Aaron said. "I believe this craft has all the potential for commercial operation. I've made my living flying business jets. This is easier. And wait until you activate the Red Box and ascend straight up in a very swift but controlled manner. I believe my boss, Captain Russell, will brief you on the specifics of the operation this afternoon."

"Yes, that's right," Matt said. "And Murray will be there as well to discuss the aerodynamic principals. Aaron will serve as your guide while you're here. No question is out of bounds."

"Great," Paula said. "The team was impressed with your staff's candor and preparation in Miami. This is a complex, unchartered area of flight, yet so far your efforts are coming through with flying colors."

Matt began to wrap things up. "Well, team, breakfast's done. Heather and Aaron, why don't you escort Paula to the hangar, so she can see Baldie for herself and meet the FAA team?

"We'll meet again after lunch for Captain Russell's briefing. He will discuss the progress of our Certification Plan, which we feel complies with the procedures in FAA Order 8110.4 and 8100.5.

"And at the end of the day, Paula, I'm sure Aaron would like to introduce you to one of the many five-star restaurants in San Pedro. Again, thank you for coming!"

After a rigorous day of tests, the teams returned to the Seabreeze. At 4 p.m. Aaron said to Paula, "I'll pick you up at 6. Wear something cool; it will still be 75 degrees. We'll walk to the restaurant."

"Terrific," Paula said. "I'll meet you here in the lobby."

They met promptly at 6 p.m., walked out of the hotel, and headed into the heart of the quaint Margaritaville-like town just two blocks from the beach and its spa resorts. Aaron pointed out the landmarks along the way. "Notice all the English signs. This was once known as Honduras, the only English colony in Central America. It gained its independence in 1981. I've been here a little over a year and enjoy the climate, people, food, friends, and, of course, the thrill of flying Baldie. Here's the restaurant — it's quaint and deserves its many stars in the guidebooks."

"Looks neat!" Paula said as they walked into the eatery.

A jovial man greeted the pair. "Welcome, Mr. Adams. Great to see you again. And with whom do I have the pleasure to serve this evening?"

"Philippe, please meet Paula."

"Welcome! Another member of the team?"

"Something like that," Aaron said.

The two were shown to a quiet table soothed by the trickle of a small waterfall in the corner. They ordered a nice bottle of wine and began to learn more about each other. Paula was also eager to learn more about Belize.

"Tomorrow you will see an environmental wonder, the Great Blue Hole just past the Belize Barrier Reef," Aaron said. "It's fantastic and for good reason draws thousands every year. Oh, and did I mention that the water's 80 degrees?"

"I'd love to see it," Paula said.

While visions of Paula in a bikini raced through Aaron's mind, he explained some of Belize's geography via a crude map written on the table paper.

He continued, "Did you know there are over 1,000 Mayan ruins here?"

"Actually, yes. I studied that in my guidebook during my flight from Houston," Paula said.

Dinner was as advertised. The sun set over the mainland as the couple walked slowly back to the Sunbreeze. They parted in the lobby. Aaron promised Paula a very exciting day tomorrow and said he hoped she would join him for another dinner in the near future.

Her eyes lit up. "I would like that very much. Thank you for a wonderful evening." She then said, "Good night" as she turned to go to her room.

There was a glint in Aaron's eyes as he turned around, smiled in delight, and headed to the veranda bar for a Baldie.

The next day came too quickly. Paula was up late answering emails and working on a course for her master's degree. She met her team for breakfast on the veranda at 7. The Flynns passed their table and wished them a successful day. Matt had to catch a flight to Tuscaloosa Alabama, where he would rent a car to travel 19 miles east to a small town called Vance, with its huge Mercedes-Benz logo dominating the horizon.

The test pilot quickly outlined the day's activities. Paula was excited, both by the adventure that awaited and by the second cup of coffee that kicked in. "OK. I signed the chit. We'll meet in the lobby in 15 minutes and walk over to the airport," Aaron said.

The Flynns' maintenance crew had already "topped her off" and rolled Baldie 3 out of the hangar.

"Thanks, Pedro. We'll take it from here," Aaron said.

The pre-flight check proceeded with a steady "check, check, check," while Paula slowly walked around the craft, its bald eagle logo on the tail gleaming in the morning sun.

The test team was ready. Paula took a seat in the front row of the passenger compartment, where she could observe the cockpit. Baldie 3 taxied out onto the runway. The local controller gave his departure clearance over the headphones. The pilot reached between the seats and activated the Red Box. In seconds, the craft hovered 100 feet above the runway. Local children and more than a few adults peered through the chain link fence to see the proud bird.

The pilot gently accelerated toward the west over the bay that separates the caye from the mainland, then turned north over the north end of Ambergris Caye and quietly and quickly rose in altitude to 1,000 feet.

"How is this possible?" Paula thought.

The craft headed east over the Barrier Reef. The pilot came over the intercom: "Ms. Frankel, please look down to the reef."

Seconds later, there it was: the Great Blue Hole, the atoll with a dark circle due to its 400-foot depth, surrounded by the light, crystal-clear azure sea.

Her heart beat quickly. She thought of what Aaron had said the night before. Fortunately she had brought a bikini.

Paula then moved up to the cockpit to check out the sensor LEDs at the engineer's station. "Captain, all systems are within tolerance," she reported.

"I know," the pilot said. "It's usually that way!"

She pulled out her laptop and made entries into her Evaluation Checklist.

As the pilot reached down to the Red Box between the seats, he called out, "Buckle up!" In a couple of seconds, Baldie 3 was climbing straight up in a horizontal position. It felt like a rocket ship taking off from Cape Kennedy.

Paula's ears popped. "Oh my God. How is this possible?" she whispered to herself. She managed to utter, "Wow! I read about this, but had no idea."

At the designated altitude, Baldie 3 covered a 20-mile figure eight course designated by the Certification Plan in record time with an average speed above 250 mph.

"This would be a hell of a ride for tourists," she thought to herself.

Per procedure, the pilot shut down the engine and restarted it while in a gentle glide mode. Several deep dives were made to test the flight-worthiness of all the control surfaces. After her ears stopped popping, Paula went to the galley to unpack lunch for the crew.

Every once in a while she would glance out of the window to see a Mayan ruin that Aaron had talked about.

The pilot announced, "There's a severe thunderstorm directly over our next course. I will circumnavigate it." Boom! The Baldie was hit by a lightning strike. The lights blinked, but otherwise all systems performed normally.

The thunderstorm veered into Baldie's flight path. In seconds, Baldie 3 was engulfed in monsoon rain and winds.

"Hold on. This could be rough!" the pilot said.

The racks of sensors shook violently, with the LEDs blinking like a Christmas tree.

After about 10 minutes — though it seemed like a lifetime — the Baldie cleared the tempest and headed home.

Paula overheard the pilot say, "In all my years, I've never felt so in control under such circumstances. This craft is amazing!" He then announced, "Team, we're headed back to San Pedro. This day of tests is completed. Be sure to log in and complete your evaluations."

Baldie 3 gently touched down in the water about 200 yards from the airport's ramp. It motored in like a giant Jet Ski, rolled up the ramp, and came to a stop in front of the hangar. The crew went inside to complete its post-flight assessments.

An hour later, Aaron arrived to escort them back to the hotel. Paula found herself staring at him, but decided to keep her feelings to herself. "It was quite a day," she thought to herself. "I learned a lot, but I have a lot more to learn about Baldie ... and myself!"

Aaron was silent as he led the team back to the hotel. When they arrived, he invited them to join him at the bar, saying, "It's time for a Baldie ... they're on me."

Two days later, during a break in the test schedule, Aaron asked Paula if she wanted to go scuba diving at the Barrier Reef. "Yes! Of course!" she said.

Up early, a bagel at Starbucks and a couple of energy drinks later, the couple walked two blocks south to the scuba shop, rented their gear, and chartered a boat for the four-hour excursion.

They frolicked in the sun and crystal blue water above one of the most beautiful reefs in the world. Aaron was tan and muscular — quite handsome with dark hair and features. Paula was stunning in her bikini, which showed off her tight body, large breasts, and trainer's buns. They swam through schools of fish and were eager to learn all they could from their guide, Captain Bob.

Before they were lobster red, they headed back to San Pedro, munching on a power bar. Paula wondered what else Aaron had in mind for this wonderful day.

As they walked back to the Sunbreeze, Paula said, "You know, we could continue this great day with one of those five-star dinners. My treat this time. That way nobody can claim you're buying the favor of a Government employee."

"You're on," Aaron said. "I'd love to."

Promptly at 6, Aaron and Paula met in the lobby and exchanged compliments about how nice the other looked. Visions of how Paula looked in her bikini ran through Aaron's mind. "Let's try a different restaurant tonight," he said.

"OK. I'm game. What's the cuisine?"

"It's a bistro. Very continental."

"Sounds great."

The couple slowly strolled down the main street, barely talking but taking in all the sights as couples and families whisked by in the preferred mode of transportation, golf carts decorated with colorful awnings.

"We're here," said Aaron.

"OK. But I don't see a restaurant," Paula replied.

"It's down this lane," he said, pointing to the right before taking her hand. "Don't worry. It's safe! I've been here before."

"Oh, that's some reassurance!" she laughed. He led her down the narrow lane. A hundred feet later they came upon small building with a red awning.

Aaron held the door open for Paula as a voice bellowed, "Monsieur Adams! So glad to see you again!"

Aaron introduced Paula to the maître d', who smiled and immediately made them feel at ease. He showed them to a cozy table for two. They ordered wine and began to talk.

"You know, Aaron," Paula began, "at our first dinner we talked about Belize, our careers, and some family background. Talking about Baldie is taboo, right?"

"Right," said Aaron.

"So, let me ask: How did you get into this project? How did you end up here?"

"That's a good question, Paula. It was pure fate. I was the pilot of an executive jet for a company that went bankrupt in Miami. One day, after landing, I saw Baldie 1 out of the corner of my eye. It was parked next to a hangar at the civil aviation terminal. After I finished my paperwork, I walked over to the craft as a man was closing the door ..."

"Hello. I'm Aaron Adams, and I couldn't help but notice your airplane."

Matt Flynn introduced himself and walked me around the aircraft while providing sketchy details. At times he seemed uncomfortable in the dialog. I guessed correctly that it could land on both terra firma and water. A very distinguished man in a pilot's uniform came up to us and said, "Hello. I'm Jim Russell. You seem interested in this craft."

I said I was and he asked about my background. I told him about my Navy flight and executive jet experience. We parted amicably. As I left, I could see the two of them talking and pointing to me.

I lost my job the next day, but Captain Russell telephoned two days later. He said, "Mr. Adams, are you interested in a co-pilot position for an experimental aircraft that has yet to be certified by the FAA?"

I thought for two milliseconds and responded: "Captain, my Navy days in the cockpit were always a challenge, but also a joy."

"I understand. I was a Marine pilot. We can swap stories later. So that's a yes?"

"That's a yes."

"Meet me at the hangar at noon tomorrow, where we can talk about details."

"Yes, sir. I'll be there."

"And the rest is history. They gave me an offer I couldn't refuse. It included months at a Central American paradise. How was a debonair bachelor to refuse?"

"I see," Paula said as she raised her eyebrows.

They clinked glasses and enjoyed a series of small dishes, each better than the one before.

"Paula, I don't see a wedding ring," Aaron said. "Now it's time for your story, please."

"I've been married to my career," Paula started. "The FAA has been wonderful. It has given me the ability to apply my engineering degree and travel to great places like this. And to meet great people like you."

Aaron wanted to kiss her that very moment. Instead, he rather bashfully said, "Thank you." He could feel himself blush and very much enjoyed the warm feeling that engulfed his body.

"I was engaged once," Paula said. "But after four months we realized it wasn't going to work. He was an astronaut and enjoyed his time in orbit more than he enjoyed his time with me."

"Sorry it didn't work out, Paula."

"I'm not! We would have eventually divorced. It was for the best. Now I'm a bachelorette enjoying the nightlife of Washington. DC has a lot to offer."

Aaron paused. "So does Belize."

"I'm coming to the same conclusion," she said. "What about your goals?"

"Well, Miami can't show me much more. I just might be happy running a fleet of Baldies between the mainland and the islands. There could be a nice lifestyle here." He looked away in a reflective manner.

"Fascinating, Aaron. I hope your dream comes true, though I'm sure it won't be without its challenges."

"You're right. Maybe that's why I'm here."

Paula paid the check as promised, and the couple returned to the resort. They said goodnight in the lobby. Aaron reached for Paula's hand, which was given freely.

"You're quite special," he said. "This was one of the best nights of my life. Thank you so much. See you early in the morning."

"I really enjoyed tonight, too, and I look forward to spending more time together," Paula said.

They went to their respective rooms to retire for the evening. As each logged on to their laptops, they thought of the other — the day, the surroundings, the possibilities for romance.

Right about midnight came a quiet knock on Paula's door. She looked through the peephole.

Aaron stood there with a bottle of 7 Star Metaxa and two snifters.

She smiled and unlatched the door. "I couldn't sleep," he whispered. ("What took you so long?" she thought to herself.)

Aaron poured two short drinks. "This will help digestion," he said as they clinked glasses and went over to the sofa.

"Paula," he said, "I tossed and turned and could only think about you. This seems to be happening so fast, but I'm smitten by you —your demeanor, intelligence, and looks — and not necessarily in that order."

Paula smiled and felt her heart rate quicken.

"I've seen you at work during the tests. We've had great meals together."

Paula was about to speak, but Aaron politely put his finger on her lips.

"Please, let me finish," he said. "When we were scuba diving and your beautiful body effortlessly glided through the water, I couldn't take my eyes off you. I hope it wasn't too obvious."

"No, you hid your emotions very well," she said. "I'm very attracted to you, Aaron. But quite frankly, I'm not sure where this will go."

Aaron gently stroked Paula's long black hair. "I'm not sure either," he said as he took another sip of cognac. "I want you in my life. It's that simple. I truly believe it's my heart speaking. I don't know how to explain it otherwise. I'm sorry for being so forward, but I believe in seizing the moment. And I haven't felt this sure of something for decades — not since I decided to be a pilot. Sorry, I'm talking your ear off."

Paula stood up, slowly took off her robe, took Aaron's hand and led him over to the bed. They sat down, embraced, kissed, and fell back into a love embrace that almost lasted until dawn. They fell asleep in each other's arms.

The alarm clock sounded at 5:45 a.m. Paula reached over and shut it off.

As they gazed into each other's eyes, Paula said, "Aaron, we need to be discrete about our relationship. I mean, outside of this room, we're strictly professionals with a job to do."

"I agree, honey. This is too beautiful to screw up. You have my promise."

Aaron rose, dressed, grabbed the cognac bottle, then paused. "On second thought, I think I'll leave it here in the cupboard," he said with a sly smile. He closed the cupboard door and glided over to the bed, passionately kissed Paula, and tiptoed out the door and down the hall.

A few minutes later, Paula got up, went over to the mirror, and admired her 41-year-old body, smiling with contentment.

"Whatever will be, will be," she said to herself before turning her focus to the Baldie tasks of the day.

Chapter 6

STUTTGART

On a star-filled night in June, Baldie 3 lifted off the runway in Miami, headed west-northwest over the Gulf of Mexico, then north to Vance, Alabama, on a flight plan authorized by the FAA. On board were the pilots, Jim Russell and Aaron Adams, along with Matt and Maggie. Matt carried a large black leather bag loaded with documents and videos. They were eager to meet officials from Mercedes-Benz to discuss a joint venture to develop and produce the Baldie. Mercedes-Benz had sent a business jet to Miami to pick up Murray for the meeting. Both craft touched down on the automobile test track around midnight. The Mercedes-Benz hostess, Angela Dicter, welcomed them in the Star Lounge.

"Thank you for coming. We've heard so much about your enterprise and are eager to learn more," she said in perfect English. "The rest of our team just crossed into U.S. airspace and should be here within an hour. You have accommodations in the VIP suite." She led the team off the elevator at the third floor. "We will have breakfast at 7 and our talks will begin at 8 with a videoconference with our chairman, Werner Von Boltz." I think you'll quickly see how serious we are about these discussions. Good night. Schlafen Sie gut!"

Breakfast came all too soon and in proportions befitting a Bavarian nobleman. The leather bag did not leave Matt's side. Angela led the team into a glass-enclosed conference room. Everything was white, black, or etched glass. "Pretty classy," Murray thought. The windows overlooked the test track and the large warehouse where Baldie spent the night. Aaron had already checked on the craft prior to breakfast and given the OK to Jim Russell. Only a couple of minutes passed before Angela led her colleagues into the room and made the introductions.

"Please meet our chief engineer, Doktor Reiner Strassburg," she started. The team shook hands with the medium-sized, light-featured gentleman with rimless spectacles. Murray was eager to meet him, as his reputation for automotive inventions and styling genius was known worldwide.

"Next I have the pleasure to introduce Herr Reinhold Timm, our factory manager here at Vance and your host," Angela continued. Engineer Timm was about 55, medium build, and bald. He had a jovial laugh and appeared quite fatherly, as though he treated every factory worker as family. During his time in Alabama he had become an accomplished bass fisherman.

Angela then introduced Horst Neumann, who grew up on the Autobahn but became Mercedes-Benz's chief pilot. He looked all the part of an astronaut. He was intrigued by the Baldie and quickly revealed that one of his life's ambitions — to pilot the Concorde — was never fulfilled.

The parties took their respective sides of the table as Angela continued, "My role at Mercedes-Benz is that of a private detective. I've made a career tracking down bogus parts and enjoy the pursuit of the truth." At age 48, she was stunningly beautiful, fluent in five languages, and a member of the Interpol inner circle of global investigators.

After the Baldie team members introduced themselves, Angela activated the touchscreen at the end of the table. Seconds later, a very distinguished gentleman seated at his desk greeted the guests with a hearty and warm, "Guten Morgen, my American friends." Werner von Boltz, the chairman, introduced himself by saying, "In my formative years, I attended the Max Planck Institute for Geophysics at Heidelberg University. I am a private pilot and keenly interested in these discussions. You have our undivided attention. I have sent you my No. 1 team, and should the discussions prove worthwhile for both parties, I invite you here to our headquarters in Stuttgart."

Maggie kept seeing images of the rocketman Wernher von Braun as he spoke. It was a brief but very sincere beginning to the meeting, and both Matt and Murray nodded approvingly. Just after the chairman signed off with a pleasant "Auf Wiedersehen," Engineer Timm took charge of the meeting.

"Our objectives are quite simple," he began. "First, we want to prove to ourselves that it does what you say it does. And second, we need to analyze the producibility of this Baldie, as you call it, or some reasonable facsimile. And based upon the documents you sent requesting this meeting, your desire is to set up a manufacturing line here in Vance. Is that correct?"

"Yes," Matt replied.

"We have reserved today and as much of tomorrow as necessary for what we call 'discovery.' You will find that we are quick learners, plus we have the benefit of the documents you have already provided. First, let me congratulate you on your patents. Needless to say, this is a big step and legitimizes the invention by the U.S. Government. Now, of course, is the biggest step — making it a profitable, commercial success."

Matt replied, "Engineer Timm, I agree. That is precisely why we are here. We feel that we have done our homework. And with the possible exception of one or two other companies, Mercedes-Benz is best positioned to apply this technology and develop a worldwide market, given your established production facilities in dozens of countries.

"Also, we came here first because the creation of new high-tech jobs in America can gain political favor, perhaps even accelerate the Baldie's acceptance in American airspace."

"Sounds logical to me, Mr. Flynn," Engineer Timm stated. "How would you like this meeting to proceed?"

Matt began, "The key is to get your team in the cockpit as soon as possible."

Heads around the table nodded in agreement.

"I propose a couple of briefings this morning. One by my brother, Murray, to describe the Red Box in general terms and its impact on any host craft. The second briefing will be by Captain Russell on the flight characteristics of something with no weight. After a brief break, we would go to the warehouse, where Aaron and Maggie would introduce you to Baldie. After lunch, weather permitting, we would commence air trials in the sequence you requested upon agreeing to this meeting. My guess is that your engineers will want to study the flight data overnight and request a couple of sorties in the morning. Of course, please feel free ask questions at any time."

Engineer Timm responded, "You know us well. After all, we're German." Consenting laughter filled the conference room. "And, of course, we'll host a true Bavarian dinner in your honor."

"Thank you. Your hospitality is most kind," Matt said. "Now, before I ask Murray to come up here, there is one thing that I must remind you of. Our meetings must be held in the strictest confidence. Outsiders must not know it takes place. We've already had run-ins with industrial spies, and there are a lot of people who want this technology. Do I have your assurance that these meetings will be treated as confidentially as Mercedes-Benz documents?" He looked directly at Angela.

"Yes, you do, Mr. Flynn," she said. "We will treat all nondisclosure documents and related materials and tests as though they were company secrets."

"Excellent," Matt said, then turned to his brother and said, "Murray, the floor is yours!"

Murray asked Maggie to pull up the first viewgraph. "Here is my outline. In less than one hour I will do my best to explain the technology and the patent arguments in layman's terms. This is not an easy task, but I will do my best. I'll take any questions. However, if the answer involves proprietary information, I will remain silent. I hope you understand."

Engineer Timm stated, "We do. The proof will be if it works reliably, economically, and under a wide variety of circumstances."

"It does, and we're here to prove it," Murray said as Matt studied the stern German faces across the table.

Murray started with a description of the atomic particle and how the whirling electrons could be harnessed to negate the downward effect of gravity on an object, regardless of how large it was.

Maggie quipped, "Believe me. I didn't understand this at first, but now I'm beginning to understand." The group chuckled.

Murray fielded a variety of questions and began to see some nodding heads around the table. He then described the key arguments of the design and process patents. It was as though he had anticipated every possible question because the room remained conspicuously silent.

"There you have it," he said as he ended his remarks with a slight smile and a quiet request for questions.

Dr. Strassburg said, "That was an excellent explanation of a very complex scenario. While I don't understand *everything* you said, I understand enough to want to participate in the tests."

A collective sigh of relief could be heard from the Baldie team.

Matt stood up and said, "Now I have the pleasure to introduce our chief pilot, Jim Russell. Jim has been with us from almost the beginning. We persuaded him to give up his seat in a 747 to help develop an experimental aircraft. He has been an inspiration to all of our crews. Captain, please take the podium."

"Thank you, Matt," Captain Russell said. "You make me feel like either a genius or a crazy barnstormer pilot. I'm not sure which." The audience chuckled.

"I've been waiting for this day for over two years, when I could report with confidence to such an august audience that the Baldie is for real and will take flight in many new venues in the near future," Captain Russell began. He asked for his first viewgraph, a photo of the cockpit controls. Maggie brought it up as Captain Russell walked over to Horst Neumann and said, "Chief Pilot Neumann, I can't wait to witness your skills, indeed, your reaction during our test flights. Your dream about the Concorde is about to be fulfilled — and much more. You have my word on it!"

The room went silent. The group could hear a race car on the test track, revving its engine.

Neumann responded, "I accept your word and will honor the opportunity."

For the next 40 minutes, Captain Russell showed a steady stream of cockpit photos and engineering data samples taken when Baldie was in a wide variety of flight conditions, from altitude storms to microbursts to water takeoffs. The audience seemed mesmerized by the videos showing Baldie in flight.

"Any questions?" he asked as he ended his remarks.

"When can we see her?" an excited Dr. Strassburg asked.

Matt's eyes met those of Engineer Timm. "How about right now?" Matt asked.

"Certainly," the production manager responded.

"Your materials are safe here," Engineer Timm said. "Let's go to the warehouse."

Matt picked up his satchel and followed his hosts as the group headed for the elevator.

Only minutes later the group arrived at the cavernous warehouse. As they entered a side door, they were greeted by Aaron Adams. "Welcome to Baldie's world. I am co-pilot Aaron Adams and, along with Maggie Flynn, I will introduce you to our very proud bird." The bright lights of the warehouse illuminated the bald eagle logo on the tail, and the pure white body glistened like never before, as if Baldie knew it was a very important day.

Aaron led the group around the craft, explaining the aerodynamic details as well as the control surfaces of a standard aircraft. He pointed out the engines which power the Baldie in the air and on the water. The Germans peppered him with questions. Aaron handled them with alacrity, like a Navy jet pilot prepared for a combat mission.

Maggie did her part explaining the inside of the Baldie 3. She showed the safety features as well as how easy it is to reconfigure it from freight to passengers and back to freight again or any combination in between. Captain Neumann took his place in the pilot's seat while Captain Russell reinforced what had just been presented.

Matt stood quietly in the background and could hear the Germans talking in the cockpit. "Keine Überraschungen hier," Dr. Strassburg was heard to say. The translation: "No surprises here." The Baldie team took this as a good sign.

Captain Neumann then opened up the floor-mounted console between the pilot's and co-pilot's seats. It was empty. He turned around, looked at Matt, and said, "Now we'll need what's in your satchel." Dr. Strassburg nodded accordingly.

Matt came forward, set the satchel down on the deck, unzipped it, and pulled out a Red Box. He handed it to Dr. Strassburg, saying, "Herr Doktor, this is why you came." The chief engineer held the Red Box on his lap and asked, "Is this all there is?"

"Yes, sir," Murray replied. You simply mount it in the console and push three switches to activate it. But *please* don't do it in here."

The group laughed heartily.

The engineer returned the Red Box to Matt with a quizzical look on his face. "How is this possible?" he repeated several times under his breath.

Angela looked at her watch and announced that lunch was being served. The party adjourned to the executive dining room.

The afternoon promised to be a real thrill for the newfound German friends.

After lunch, Matt announced, "Baldie 3 has been moved to the test track." The group pressed up against the window to see the craft gleaming in the Alabama sun. "Shall we join him and continue with our day?"

On the tarmac, Matt explained the sequence of tests, the monitoring equipment, and the participants for each assessment. A total of four flights were planned for the afternoon. The first flight would have Captain Russell pilot the craft with Captain Neumann in the co-pilot's seat. Baldie would do a series of figure eights in a prescribed course over a 20-mile square south of Vance in a very sparsely populated area. Three racks of equipment specified by Mercedes-Benz were installed behind the cockpit and monitored by two technicians. Matt dropped the Red Box onto the console, wished the crew good luck, and with the rest of the team left the craft. The portside hatch was closed.

Soon Baldie's engines could be heard revving up. The group returned to a test area set up just outside the warehouse. As they squinted against the afternoon sun, Baldie slowly rose above the test track. The craft hovered at 100 feet for about 10 seconds and then, almost flying saucer–like, shot straight up to become a silver speck against the deep blue sky. While the teams awaited the return of Baldie, Matt and Murray described the remaining three flight tests.

The second test had Captain Neumann at the controls with Aaron Adams as the co-pilot. A series of airframe flight tests were conducted to prove control under a variety of conditions.

The third test was performed under the control of Captain Russell, with Captain Neumann in the co-pilot's seat. Dr. Strassburg sat at the engineer's station. Engineer Timm was also aboard, with Captain Adams providing detailed explanations. This flight included a series of roll maneuvers and a dangerous dead stall. Captain Russell shut off the engines and Baldie responded by remaining in place, perfectly horizontal. The safety parachute did not need to be deployed. Captain Russell restarted the engines and Baldie 3 responded with a steady increase in velocity on a true north heading. Engineer Timm's face visibly relaxed as he continued to pelt Adams with questions about the materials used to construct the craft. He was an intellectual sponge, and Adams was up to the task.

With the third test completed, Baldie 3 slowly approached the test track from the west. It landed with virtually no sound and taxied to the warehouse tarmac. A minute later the hatch opened, the stairs deployed, and Dr. Strassburg came out, waving to the warehouse. A rare smile spread across his face.

At 4 that afternoon, the fourth flight test took place. It was a water landing and takeoff at a nearby lake. A group of nude teenagers scattered for the woods, their sunbathing interrupted, as Baldie glided down onto the surface. Captain Russell relinquished the controls to Captain Neumann, saying, "OK, Horst, let's motor around the lake a couple turns for you to get comfortable, and then take off. You'll see how easy it is to manage this seaplane." Dr. Strassburg found it comforting that every body of water could also be a landing spot. "This must be the safest craft to ever fly," he thought to himself.

A short time later, at the end of the lake, Captain Neumann pushed the throttle forward. Baldie immediately raised up as to hydroplane, skipping across the still waters. Seconds later, Captain Russell nodded to Captain Neumann, who pulled back on the wheel. Baldie responded just as the

Baldie team knew he would, clearing the tree-lined shore by 50 feet. In the distance the teenagers could be seen heading back to the water. He chuckled under his breath as he thought to himself, "They must have thought Baldie was a UFO!"

After about 10 minutes the technicians notified Captain Neumann that all the flight data had been captured. It was time to end the test flight and return to the Mercedes-Benz plant. The sprawling, gleaming white facility soon appeared over the horizon. Engineer Timm radioed ahead to stop the automobile testing to allow Baldie to land. This time a large group of employees was gathered on the south parking lot, awaiting its arrival and wondering what Mercedes-Benz was up to now. Baldie circled the track at 100 feet and gently touched down on the tarmac by the warehouse. Captain Neumann could be seen at the controls. The pilot's window opened and a thumbs-up sign was given. Loud, spontaneous applause resulted. As the test team departed the craft, additional cheers filled the pines ringing the plant. A security detachment pulled up and cordoned off Baldie from curious onlookers. Matt met the team at the doorway to the warehouse.

"Well, Skipper Neumann, what do you think?" he asked.

Neumann reflected a moment, then said, "I'll reserve judgment until after I see the data, but I can tell you from a flight experience, the Concorde could not have been any better." He smiled as he led his team into the main building.

Matt whispered to Murray, "You can bet they'll call Stuttgart tonight." Murray nodded.

As the group gathered together, Angela invited the Baldie team to the Bavarian dinner as promised. "See you at 7 for cocktails in the VIP lounge," she said. "We'll have a little tour of our automobile museum."

"We'll be there," said Matt, who then instructed Aaron and Maggie to bring him the Red Box and secure Baldie for the evening.

Matt asked the team to join him in his room for a short debriefing. Captain Russell reported that all flights went as planned, and that the Germans should be reviewing data with no anomalies.

"Perfect," Matt replied. "Murray, any comment?"

"No. I believe we're on course for some serious negotiations. I firmly believe they want to seize the initiative and not be upstaged by Boeing or any other American company. After all, we're giving them the first right of refusal. In this case it's a multibillion-dollar decision."

"Aaron, what about you? Any comment?" Matt asked.

"Only that they really appreciate that Baldie can land anywhere," Aaron replied. "And Engineer Timm already has some production methods in mind."

"Good. Thanks."

Matt then turned to his sister-in-law and said, "Maggie, what about you? Your thoughts, please."

"Well, they have seen the technology in the form of an aircraft. If the data holds, and I think it will, I believe they have a much larger endeavor in mind. After all, they manufacture buses and trucks around the world. This could change transportation as we know it for centuries. The chairman sent his top people for a reason."

"Good points, Maggie, as usual. Thanks," Matt said. "OK, guys, let's freshen up and be ready for round three, I mean dinner." Everyone chuckled and then dispersed.

Matt approached his brother and said, "Murray, I think they will invite us to Stuttgart. Did you bring the adapter kit?"

"Yes. I have it in my room."

"Great. I really believe it will seal the deal."

Promptly at 7, the Baldie team entered the Mercedes-Benz Museum. They were handed a glass of champagne while a tall, striking, blond woman escorted them around the automobiles, each an engineering achievement of some merit.

After 20 minutes, Angela appeared to usher the team up to the VIP room for dinner. The dining room was decorated with gaily colored ribbons and hand-carved Bavarian crafts. German wines and beers were offered by the hosts. Dr. Strassburg headed one large circular table and Captain Neumann the other. Jim Russell and Aaron Adams were seated on either side of Captain Neumann. They joked that it was the pilots' table. The other table had Matt and Murray flanking the chief engineer. Maggie was between Murray and Angela. Engineer Timm and three of his key foremen completed the group. The fare was traditional German cuisine, which was fresh and tasty. Matt joked that it had been flown in for the occasion.

As the group enjoyed their entrees, an envelope was delivered to Dr. Strassburg. He opened it, took a quick glance at its contents, and sealed it without showing any emotion. Matt's eyes met Murray's as they silently surmised that all technical data had passed inspection. Engineer Timm entertained the group with some of his stories about how a Bavarian learns bass fishing from local Alabamans.

As dessert was being served, Dr. Strassburg stood up, tapped his glass with a spoon, and waited for silence.

"Mr. Flynn," he began, "I want to sincerely thank you for bringing your team and Baldie to Mercedes-Benz. In my four decades of service to this company, I have been privileged to be part of many automotive firsts. Now it appears I may be party to a whole new chapter in our corporate life, one that involves Baldie. Your proud bird has passed every test we could possibly give it. As you know, we have the data and will gladly share it with your engineers."

Matt nodded his approval.

"Chairman von Boltz has sent his personal invitation for your team to join him in Stuttgart for the next phase of discussions. I fervently hope you will accept his invitation."

All eyes were on Matt as he rose with his toasting glass in hand.

He paused, then said, "I believe I speak for the Baldie team when I say I accept the chairman's gracious invitation."

The group stood up as Murray led the simple toast: "To Baldie. May he serve humanity in so many ways for so many years to come. Cheers!"

Champagne never tasted so good to Maggie. She wiped a tear from her eye and caught Aaron doing the same.

"Very good," Dr. Strassburg said, addressing Matt. "Another plane will be here tomorrow morning so that you and Murray can fly separately."

Matt replied, "Thank you, Herr Doktor Strassburg. I firmly believe that this endeavor will be fruitful and long lasting for humanity. My brother's toast was quite appropriate. Now, before we adjourn to the cigar bar, may I have a short word with you, Captain Neumann, and Engineer Timm?"

"Of course," Dr. Strassburg said. "Please follow me to my private office." Matt picked up his satchel and followed his host into a spacious office lined with pictures of Mercedes-Benz race cars.

With the four men seated at a round oak table, Matt reached into the satchel. He carefully put a bracket the size of an ammunition box with three lead wires on the table, then asked if they knew what it was.

"It looks like a mounting bracket subsystem," Engineer Timm said.

Captain Neumann grinned from ear to ear. "I know what it is!" he said.

Dr. Strassburg asked his chief pilot, "Well? Don't keep us in suspense!"

Captain Neumann replied, "Herr Doktor, Mr. Flynn is offering to mount a Red Box in one of the Gulfstream jets headed to Stuttgart as a genuine proof of concept."

He turned to Matt and asked, "Am I right?"

"Horst, in English we say, 'You nailed it!'" Matt replied. "Yes, that is exactly what I propose. Indeed, I envision landing vertically on the grass behind your employee cafeteria, or would you rather we land in the fish pond? Clearly, we've done a little research on Google Earth."

The Germans were stunned. The very thought that the chairman could see the Baldie land for himself was, in a word, earthshaking.

Matt continued, "Your plane would be treated like a helicopter landing at your headquarters. The flight plan can be filed. There should be no alarms to the authorities."

Captain Neumann, who had already flown a Baldie twice during the day, liked the proposal. "I think this can be arranged," he said with exuberance in his voice.

"Very good," Matt said. "My suggestion is that we wait until tomorrow afternoon before we leave. This will give my factory manager, Don Carlos Fuentes, time to bring the second Red Box. In this way Baldie 3 can return to Miami and the new Red Box can be installed in Captain Neumann's plane. You know we're on thin ice here because any airframe modifications require certification. However, because this is termed an 'experimental flight' and we're flying over the Atlantic at low altitude at night, the safety issues should be minimal. Indeed, we can fly through the Strait of Gibraltar and turn north over the Alps. If anybody will approve such an overflight, it will be the Italians and the Swiss."

"Captain Neumann, you make the decision," Dr. Strassburg said. Neumann quickly assessed the situation.

"Matt is right," he said. "It minimizes any danger to the crew or people on the ground below. Indeed, similar to the Baldie design, our jet's engines are mounted on the tail, enabling a water landing if necessary. I believe the risks are minimal."

"Horst, I'll support you on this," Dr. Strassburg said. "The impact upon our boss will be immediate."

They shook hands and went down the hall to the impromptu cigar bar while Matt called Don Carlos on his cell phone to relate the plan.

The party soon became quite comfortable in the room's leather chairs while enjoying quality cigars and cognac. All the while, the Red Box sat patiently in the satchel next to Matt, waiting for its next assignment.

The next morning, strong coffee cleared the mind to focus on the day's events. After breakfast, there was an intense meeting with Engineer Timm and his staff to review production options while minimizing the impact upon the Vance facility. The options were prioritized and staff was assigned to cost them out. Don Carlos arrived with the Red Box and an encrypted parts list on a flash drive. It was a very productive session.

Shortly after lunch, the now joint Baldie-German team wished Aaron and Maggie a bon voyage as Baldie 3 taxied to the test track for its liftoff and flight to Miami. Soon afterward, the second executive jet landed. Don Carlos supervised the installation of the Red Box in Captain Neumann's aircraft. At sunset both aircraft took off, with Matt and Captain Russell in one and Murray and Aaron Adams in the other. Captain Neumann activated the Red Box. Within minutes his craft caught up to the other executive jet as it left America, headed to Europe. Matt, who was stretched out in the back, could hardly sleep. He had dreamed of this scenario for more than a year, and now it was coming true. He knew that real-life demonstrations were more powerful than the physics explanations that made the Red Box function. It was a calculated risk that he hoped was about to pay off.

Both planes were approaching European airspace five hours later. Murray's plane took the traditional route over southern France, while Matt's plane flew directly over the Strait of Gibraltar and turned north over remote northern Italy and then Switzerland. Captain Neumann knew the territory like the back of his hand. He approached Mercedes-Benz' headquarters in Unterturkheim, an eastern suburb of Stuttgart, over the fields from the southeast. Angela radioed ahead to the facility security force to cordon off the parkland behind the employee cafeteria. It was now 7:26 in the morning, with a bright sunrise reflecting off the gleaming white Gulfstream.

At 300 feet and a final approach profile, Captain Neumann spoke. "Captain Russell, I believe you should execute the final descent. It must be perfect."

Captain Russell responded. "Yes sir, Captain. I have the control."

Startled employees pushed against the cafeteria windows. The drapes on the fourth floor conference room were opened to provide a clear view for the executive staff. Von Boltz was surrounded by his principal officers.

Captain Russell shut down the engine while simultaneously reducing the Red Box energy level with his left hand to create an eerily silent, controlled descent onto the green lawn. Angela could be heard on her cell phone, telling von Boltz's staff, "The Eagle has landed." Captain Russell appreciated the reference to the moon landing in July 1969.

As the crew shut down the craft, they received word that Murray's plane had landed at the airport. Captain Russell disengaged the Red Box and handed it to Matt. There were wide grins as the pilots shook hands. Angela opened the hatch, lowered the steps, and stepped onto the platform. She looked up to the fourth-floor window, crisply saluted, and stepped down. The others followed her into the building. Matt, who was carrying the satchel, remotely closed the hatch and armed the security systems. He felt confident the day would go well for the Baldie team.

Angela accompanied the team members, who were whisked away to their hotel in limousines. As they checked in, Angela said, "Please rest now. We have a full afternoon. Please enjoy lunch here. I will pick you up at 1." Matt nodded in agreement.

While the Baldie team enjoyed a relaxing morning, back at Mercedes-Benz headquarters three teams were very busy: technical, production, and financial. Dr. Strassburg seemed to enjoy his role as overseer of the process. Promptly at 11, the teams reported their findings. The results: no test anomalies, three potential production lines, and margins within Mercedes-Benz's guidelines for a new vehicle/airship model. Dr. Strassburg, Chief Pilot Neumann, Bernhard Holzmann, the director of global marketing, and two senior board members were invited to lunch with Chairman von Boltz.

The chairman quickly asked, "What am I missing here? A revolutionary technology falls from the sky into my back yard, and we have the opportunity to change the transportation structure on the planet. Am I wrong? Does the data back up their so-called 'Baldie'?" One by one, the group validated the data and their findings.

"So what you're telling me is that this is real and deserves our undivided attention," he said.

A chorus of "Yes, sirs" followed.

"What about this guy Flynn? Is he honest? Is he who he said he is? The patents check out, but what about the man and his brother, the genius astrophysicist?"

Bernhard Holzmann spoke up. "Sir, Angela has been on this case for three months. There are no negatives."

Von Boltz turned to his chief engineer. "Dr. Strassburg, what about the science? It is sustainable? Can we build a long-term business on this technology?"

Dr. Strassburg responded, "Sir, it's not a single business, but many. Society as we know it will change in less than a generation."

"Very well," von Boltz said. "So you are unanimous in your desire to see a successful conclusion to our negotiations."

Another round of "Yes, sirs" filled the room — this time at a higher volume.

The chairman was pensive for a minute. "Angela, let's proceed with this afternoon's meetings and make arrangements for a first-class dinner at the museum."

"Yes, sir," she replied. "I'm off to the hotel now to retrieve our guests." The group arose with their coffee cups and followed von Boltz to the window. They looked down at the executive jet on the grass. No one spoke. The chairman broke the silence.

"Yes, the Eagle has landed. But if my dream comes true, billions of people will benefit from its wings. This meeting is over. Go make it happen." You could almost hear steps landing in unison as the team dispersed into their own domains.

With German punctuality, Angela greeted the Baldie team in the lobby at 1 p.m.

"Chairman von Boltz sends his warm greetings for successful discussions. I will not be with you during the meeting, as I will be arranging a special dinner at the museum in your honor tonight."

"We're rested and ready for today's events. Thank you!" Matt said.

Twenty minutes later, the Baldie team was escorted up to the rarified air of the inner sanctum of the fourth floor. Though the building was 16 stories tall, the chairman felt that was too far away from his roots, the factory floor.

Matt carried the satchel into the conference room, which was now crowded with support staff. The Baldie team took its place at the table across from their newfound friends from Vance, Alabama. About two minutes later, the chairman took his seat at the end of the table and said, "Mr. Flynn, this is a huge organization. We build many things. But right now you have our undivided attention. Incredibly, there is an executive jet on our lawn. This is rather a unique way to visit someone. Why are you here? What is your proposal?"

"Dr. von Boltz," Matt began in a clear and powerful voice, "my mission is to combine the best of American ingenuity with the best German production technologies to change the way people move on this planet. You see, I have a dream, and I'm here to ask your help in fulfilling it."

The chairman nodded his approval.

"Thank you, sir, for this forum. We will try not to disappoint you and your staff," Matt said as he took a Red Box out of his satchel and placed it on the table in front of the chairman. "Thanks to my brother, Murray, we are here today. He has invented a small device with big consequences. It turns anything into something that wants to escape gravity and leave this planet. The patents confirm its technology, and the jet on your back lawn confirms its application."

"Herr Chairman," Matt continued, "I have driven Mercedes vehicles for over 30 years. I believe in your design, engineering and production methodologies that ensure a quality vehicle.

"Because I'm a believer, I only need 10 minutes to state my case. Here are 10 folders which summarize what I am about to propose. I'm not a cocky

American who flaunts his technology and independence. On the contrary, I come to you in partnership to jointly apply my brother's genius on behalf of mankind.

"Your people have undoubtedly digested the data from our test fights in Alabama. Any problems?"

"No," Chairman von Boltz responded.

"Good."

Matt went over to the Red Box and patted it. "The jet down there is there because of this. Is that clear?"

"Yes," the chairman replied.

The Baldie team was ready for Matt's 10 minutes of fame. He continued, "You produce cars, trucks, and buses all over this planet. Why not the Baldie?"

The Mercedes-Benz team nodded in agreement.

"We came to you first for your expertise in all departments," Matt said. "We feel Vance, Alabama, is the ideal place to start Baldie production because it creates American jobs, which our president can leverage in his re-election campaign.

"We also feel the United States would be the logical and largest first market, with its crowded expressways and lots of discretionary income. Plus, the FAA is close to certifying Baldie for use over American airspace.

"What's more, as your lawyers have no doubt found out, our patent claims are not only 'iron-proof,' but global in impact.

"And, finally, we want to start with a service between Caribbean islands, which is safe and profitable. I believe your accountants will confirm that it only takes a franchise with three Baldies to be profitable."

Bernhard Holzmann interrupted. "Mr. Flynn, we have already verified that. You are correct."

"Thank you," Matt said. "Therefore, I propose that you modify one of your SUV production lines at Vance to produce the Baldie under an initial license agreement. Mercedes-Benz would have the exclusive rights for three years, which would be renegotiable annually. After three years, a second production facility would be authorized elsewhere in America. This would give you a three-year head start to produce the Baldie anywhere on earth. The production of the Red Box would remain with us both in Miami and our secondary location. We would be incentivized to keep up with your production schedule.

"The second element of our proposal is the creation and operation of a pilot's school in Miami. Trained pilots are required for every Baldie.

"The third element is the development of a global marketing campaign, complete with a budget by geographic region.

"And the fourth element is your testimony before U.S. Government officials like the FAA or even President Werner. You see, we believe that Baldie's job-creation ability could be an important campaign theme in the president's re-election bid."

"It seems, Mr. Flynn, that you've done your homework," Chairman von Boltz said.

"Oh, and there's one more thing," Matt said. "We request your help in determining the next applications after the Baldie. Who knows? Someday there could be a personal Baldie."

Broad smiles filled the room.

Holzmann spoke up. "This is very ambitious," he said. "Who's going to pay for all this?"

Matt replied, "We've invested almost $10 million in this enterprise to date. My estimate, and it's only an estimate because I don't know the costs involved in modifying the production facility, would be an approximately $20 million commitment by Mercedes-Benz over the next two years."

He turned to the company's leader and added, "But, Chairman von Boltz, it shouldn't cost you a Mark in the long run."

Every German eyebrow was raised.

"You see," Matt continued, "I plan to charge the U.S. Government $1 billion tax-free annually for the license. Should we come to terms, we offer 10 percent of this to Mercedes-Benz — annually."

With this Matt placed a dozen copies of a bound proposal in the middle of the conference table.

"They're in German, of course," he said. As the documents were distributed to the participants, Matt walked over to the windows, looked down, paused, and in a slow, low tone said, "Oh, and we'll move your airplane for free."

Laughter filled the room.

The chairman said, "Thank you. We will review the document and reconvene at 4 this afternoon. Angela has arranged a secure room — no bugs! — for your team. And please plan to be our guests for dinner at the museum."

Promptly at 4 p.m., the same parties returned to the conference room.

Chairman von Boltz took his place at the head of the table.

"Mr. Flynn, I congratulate your team on its accomplishments to date," he said. "You have certainly impressed my team with your technology and business acumen. The fact that you came here first is truly appreciated. We will implement your plan in two phases. First, we will develop a fully priced production plan for the Vance plant within five months. We will need the full cooperation of your team and probably some key suppliers."

"Yes, sir. You will have it," Matt said.

"Second, once the board approves the plan, we will modify the facilities within six months, with the goal of producing the first Baldie for rollout within the next six months. We will need your assurance that you can manufacture the Red Box to meet our full production. Is this timetable agreeable with you and your team?"

Matt looked at Murray, who nodded his approval. The other Baldie team members also nodded.

"Mr. Chairman, it appears unanimous," Matt said. "We accept your plan and timetable with the rollout during the summer, when the president starts his re-election campaign."

"Excellent," the chairman responded. "We will execute a licensing agreement and form three teams: production, marketing, and pilot school. I will fund these efforts through the end of the year and welcome your return for a detailed status report at that time."

"Yes, sir. I look forward to delivering that report," Matt replied.

"Very well. If there is no other business, this meeting is adjourned. I will see you at dinner."

The teams shook hands across the table, voiced congenialities, and departed.

At 6:45 p.m. two Mercedes-Maybach Pullman cars pulled up in front of the Baldie team's hotel. The doorman let Angela out of the first car. She went into the lobby and greeted the team. Matt got into the first car and Murray into the second. The cars quickly sped away for the 15-minute drive to the museum.

"It's a shame we only have 45 minutes for the tour," Murray remarked when he saw the museum's stunning architecture. The museum's rounded, futuristic shape resembled the Guggenheim Museum in New York City.

"I agree," Captain Russell said.

Promptly at 7:30, Angela herded the team into the elevator, and they headed for the fifth-floor dining room set up for the occasion. As they got off the elevator, they were greeted by Chairman von Boltz.

"Mr. Flynn, where is your satchel?" he asked.

Matt smiled as he turned around to show the knapsack on his back, which blended into his sport coat and wasn't immediately obvious.

Everyone chuckled.

Soon afterward, the guests were treated to a sumptuous dinner followed by a seemingly endless succession of champagne toasts. Maggie nudged Murray and said, "I'm glad you're not driving, dear."

At 9:30 the Pullman pulled up to the hotel. Matt shook Angela's hand and said, "Thank you so much. This has been an incredible day."

"I agree," she replied. "Quite incredible. I'm so glad it worked out the way it did. This should be quite a program!"

"Agreed," Matt said.

"I will pick you up at 8 tomorrow morning," she said as he got into the Maybach.

"Guten Morgen, Herr Flynn," was Angela's greeting the next morning. "We have two cars — one for you and your team to return to Unterturkheim, and another for Murray to return to the airport. I hope this is acceptable."

"It sure is. Vielen Dank," Matt replied.

Murray's Maybach sped off to the airport with the other occupants already in the car. As Matt placed his backpack into the other car and closed the trunk, a shot rang out. A bullet pierced the trunk, narrowly missing the Red Box and the gas tank.

Matt looked up. On the roof across the street from the hotel he caught a glimpse of a rifle barrel and a scope. He shouted to the team inside the car, "Heads down!" Everyone fell to the floor. Matt jumped into the car as Angela hopped into the front passenger seat and yelled, "Schnell, schnell!" The driver pushed the Maybach to the maximum as it raced away from the hotel. A block later, a green Citroën bumped the Maybach to force it off the road. Fortunately, the 6,500-pound vehicle didn't budge. Angela, always the detective, caught four of the six license plate numbers on the Citroën as it tried once again to run the Maybach off the road, but failed. She pulled out her gun and got a couple shots off at the tires, but the car kept on its pursuit.

The race continued. Five blocks later, the Maybach turned into the Mercedes-Benz parking lot. The green Citroën sped away. Angela was already talking to Interpol headquarters via cell phone to identify the vehicle.

As they pulled into the garage, Angela hopped out and opened the passenger door. "Is everyone all right?"

"Yes, we're fine," came a reply.

"Good. Please follow me," she said as she led Matt and the team to the cafeteria of the compound. "You will be safe here. Mr. Flynn, please prepare your crew for takeoff." Everyone scrambled outside to the lawn behind the cafeteria and took their places inside the Baldie.

"It's clear that this technology has global implications. We will get to the bottom of this," Angela said. She placed several calls while Captains Neumann and Russell prepared the executive jet for flight. Matt then inserted the Red Box into the host console and activated it.

Only two minutes later, the Gulfstream was slowly rising over the lawn, turning on a south-southwest heading out of Stuttgart. Captain Russell heard over the headset that the other plane was airborne en route to Miami.

Matt checked his seat belt and settled back into the soft leather seat with a smile of satisfaction on his face which camouflaged his concern about the most recent attempt to steal the Red Box. As he fell asleep over the Atlantic, he resolved to improve the security measures at both production facilities.

Chapter 7

PARIS

One month after the meetings in Stuttgart, the National Gendarmerie in Paris called Angela.

"We have spotted the green Citroën. It matches the license plate number you gave us," an officer reported.

"Great," she said. "I'll get a flight and be there by noon." By 12:30 she was in a command center, briefing the police about the incident and why Mercedes-Benz was so interested in determining who was behind this ring of thieves so intent on getting a Red Box. She told them about the attempted theft in Miami and how the suspects' trail had alerted the police in Hong Kong.

"Mercedes-Benz will have a lot at stake with this technology," she explained. "The impact will be global, including right here in Paris, and sooner rather than later. We believe the Chinese consider it a 'game-changer' to restart their stalled economy. It's that important."

Within an hour roadblocks were set up on the seven main arteries leading out of Paris.

All eyes in the command center were fixed on a large display which showed the plaza in front of the Musée du Louvre.

"There it is!" and officer in the back of the room shouted.

Two police cars were immediately called into action to converge on the Citroën and corner it. The Citroën used the sidewalk and knocked down traffic signs, narrowly missing a fire hydrant as the chase began.

At high speed the three cars headed west on the Rue de Rivoli along the north side of the Jardin des Tuileries toward the Place de la Concorde. They turned onto the Champs-Élysées, darting in and out of traffic with the sirens blaring. The cars swerved around the Arc de Triomphe, past the Charles de Gaulle — Étoile onto Avenue Kléber.

One shot was fired at the tire of the Citroën but missed. More police cars were alerted to the chase.

The cars raced toward the Trocadéro and the Palais de Chaillot. At high speed they fishtailed as they entered Rue le Tasse and then crossed over the Seine onto Quai Branly, headed south past the Eiffel Tower.

A roadblock was established a few blocks west of the École Militaire. Another police car joined the chase as the cars turned left onto Boulevard de Grenelle. Near the Institut Pasteur, the convoy sped up Rue de Vaugirard, headed northeast. Barely missing pedestrians, the speeding cars crossed over Boulevard Raspail and headed straight for the Palais du Luxembourg, where a roadblock forced the Citroën to turn into the courtyard parking lot.

The car spun around and came to a stop. Two darkly clad occupants fled on foot, firing handguns at the police. The police returned fire and launched two teargas canisters as frightened tourists lay upon the pavement behind fountains.

The two suspects ran into Luxembourg Garden, where they confronted the police and then turned the guns on each other rather than be caught.

The command center was notified of the outcome. Angela hoped clues would be found that would lead authorities to the brains behind the attempted Red Box thefts.

"Gentlemen, you've done a great service," she said. "I look forward to a full report about the suspects. I'm determined to get to the bottom of this."

"We are, too," said the precinct captain on duty.

Angela phoned her boss at Mercedes-Benz and updated him on the situation. She returned to Stuttgart that evening. As she got off the plane, she received an email that read, "Nice work. Take a vacation in Miami and help the Flynns beef up their security."

Chapter 8

OVAL OFFICE

Armed with the patents, successful FAA certification tests, and a preliminary production plan at Mercedes-Benz, the Flynns decided the time was right to put a full-court press on the decision-makers in Washington, D.C.

In February Matt briefed Secretary of the Treasury Adam Aurum and Clayton Feller, the nation's chief economist, about the potential impact of the Red Box on America and beyond its shores.

Murray briefed senior officials at the Department of Defense, including the director of the Defense Advanced Research Project Agency (DARPA) in Roslyn, Virginia. DARPA funds new technologies like the ARPANET, the foundation of the Internet, and the latest aircraft. Leading physicists were brought in to analyze the Red Box and Murray's arguments. He prevailed.

The DARPA director was so impressed that he called his counterparts in the intelligence community to host a special classified briefing by Matt and Murray at CIA Headquarters in Langley, Virginia, a D.C. suburb.

Maggie, Heather, and Aaron helped Matt create a briefing, including videos of Baldie 3's successful tests in Belize.

Matt called Paula at the FAA and requested her assistance in scheduling a briefing for the president. She said she would do her best. At the same time, José Diaz, the facility manager in Miami, called his high school friend, Rita Morales, the appointment secretary for President Werner, and requested a "once-in-a-lifetime" favor of an hour briefing in March. And Matt called Angela Dicter to alert Chairman von Boltz and his staff about a potential meeting with the president. He asked that a few briefing charts be made up about the Mercedes-Benz commitment to the project and the "Made in America" production plans.

Unbeknownst to Matt and Murray, some of the parties they briefed were also calling the White House.

Early in March, Matt was in his office at the Miami facility when José appeared in the doorway and bellowed, "We're on!" as he gave the thumbs-up sign.

Matt turned around from the computer, smiled, and asked, "When?"

"In two weeks, on March 26," José replied.

Within minutes Matt was on the phone with Angela.

"I sure hope the chairman can make it!" Angela said. She told Matt she would get back to him by the end of the day.

At 6 that evening Matt's phone rang. José, Murray, and Maggie raced down the hall from their offices and crowded around the entrance to Matt's office.

Matt could see the telephone number from Germany. He picked up the phone and said, "Hello, Angela. I hope you have some good news for me."

"I sure do," Angela said. "There will be three of us coming — the chairman, Dr. Strassburg, and yours truly."

Matt gave the thumbs-up sign to his three eager colleagues, who immediately gave each other high fives.

"Oh, and Matt," Angela continued, "We will go to the Vance plant earlier that week to get a full briefing on the production readiness plans. Chairman von Boltz wants to be ready for any possible question from the president."

"Perfect," Matt said. "I'll call you later this week with the arrangements for Washington. Goodbye, Angela, and thanks a million — I mean a billion!"

The next day the attendance list was faxed to the White House for security purposes, and the Baldie team manned their battle stations to prepare for the big event. Murray even got a haircut.

On March 25 the Baldie team — American and German — practiced the briefing in a conference room at the Willard Hotel. Murray was in charge of the Red Box. At dinner that evening, Reiner Strassburg briefed his colleagues about the production preparations in Vance. All were in high spirits. If the team was nervous, it wasn't apparent.

An hour and a half before the briefing on March 26, the Baldie team walked the three blocks from the hotel to the White House. They were screened in security and met by Rita, who escorted them to the conference room near the Oval Office.

"You have 20 minutes to set up," she said. "Good luck and please give my best to José."

"We sure will," Matt said.

The team — Matt, Murray, Maggie, Chairman von Boltz, Dr. Strassburg, and Angela — took its place on one side of the long mahogany conference table. Five minutes later, Rita ushered in Adam Aurum, Secretary of Defense Jefferson Palmer, CIA Director Reid Burnham, and Campaign Manager Bill Cavanaugh, who took their seats on the other side of the table. Several staff members lined the wall.

The door opened and President Werner entered briskly, took his seat at the head of the table, and said, "Mr. Flynn, I believe you have something very interesting to show us. Please proceed."

After introducing his team, Matt began, "Mr. President, we are here today to introduce you and your team to our technology, which we believe will in many ways impact our country and even the globe. I do not make this statement lightly. First, we will introduce you to the Baldie via a short video. Then we will describe the Red Box. The third portion of the briefing describes our 'Made in America' production plans, and in the last 20 minutes I'll summarize our proposal's impact on the nation."

Matt asked Maggie to start the video showing Captain Russell walking around the Baldie, describing its primary features, and then narrating actual flight footage. It's fair to say that the audience was stunned when Baldie took off like a flying saucer.

The president turned to CIA Director Burnham and asked, "How is that possible?"

The director said nothing, but pointed to the Red Box Murray was lifting onto the table. "Sir," Matt said, "my brother Murray will now describe the Red Box in layman's terms — or at least he'll try." The audience chuckled. Staffers leaned forward to see this magic box. In 12 minutes Murray summarized the physics, described the patent claims, and provided a video walk-through of the production process at the Miami facility. There were no questions.

At this point in the briefing Matt proudly introduced Chairman von Boltz. The chairman looked around the room and then spoke directly to the president.

"President Werner, by my presence here today and the concurrence of my board of directors, Mercedes-Benz is committed to making the Red Box and the Baldie international success stories. And we want to start in Alabama."

Chairman von Boltz then introduced Reiner Strassburg, who showed a short video of the Vance plant and walked the audience through the Baldie production process. He ended by saying, "Chairman von Boltz and I were in Vance two days ago. We are ready. We are committed. The first Baldie can roll off the assembly line in 11 months."

Matt stood up and went to the end of the table and asked Maggie to bring up a viewgraph. He said, "Mr. President and distinguished guests, this chart summarizes why we believe you should approve the proposal we presented to Secretary Aurum last week." He read each bullet:

- Creates new industries
- Strengthens the dollar
- Improves America's balance of trade
- Increases tax revenue
- Helps balance the budget
- Earns bipartisan congressional support
- Revamps the national transportation infrastructure
- Puts the country back into space
- Enables new warfare concepts
- Saves fuel
- Saves the environment

"Maggie, please show the last slide," Matt said.

On the screen was a simulated lapel button with a blue and red outer ring and a large red "1M" on a white background in the center. Some of the audience immediately knew what it meant.

Matt walked back to his seat next to the president and handed him a button, saying, "Sir, we believe this button will have the same impact as the 'I like Ike' button more than a half-century ago. It represents the million jobs to be created by this technology." Buttons were handed out around the table.

The president looked directly at his campaign manager, Bill Cavanaugh, and said, "Mr. Flynn, I will review your proposal and get back to you within a week. This presentation has made my day, perhaps even my year."

The meeting adjourned.

The Flynns hosted a Texas steak dinner that evening.

Chapter 9

HONG KONG

Immediately after the theft of the Red Box in South Miami, Matt retained two Chinese detectives who happened to be vacationing in Miami. He knew the lead detective, Chin Chin Po, from college, where she had graduated with honors in criminology. Detective Po, who resembled the Chinese actress Li Bingbing, had earned a reputation for solving tough cases. Her assistant, Tinshin Wei, was an internationally known database researcher who quickly identified and tracked criminal suspects. She, too, was a petite woman with delicate features.

In a telephone conversation with Matt, Detective Po asked, "Could this be an inside job? The ninjas knew all about your facility. Have you fired any employees recently?"

Matt replied, "Yes, we fired a Chinese software engineer two months ago for smoking marijuana in the parking lot. He had access to the security codes and knew every square foot of this facility."

Matt paused, then asked Detective Po, "Why do you think they took a Red Box? If they try to open it, it will self-destruct. What government needs the technology to bolster their economy and gain military advantage?"

They both answered simultaneously: "China."

Over the next week, the detectives searched their databases of Miami International Airport's entry records and rental car registries. Soon they zeroed in on a short list of recent visa entries who had theft records or were known felons.

The detectives actually enjoyed serving as female Sherlock Holmeses on this intriguing case. Their Type A personalities had them driving around Miami, checking leads. At the fourth apartment complex they stopped at, the manager reported that two Chinese renters checked out last week. He said he overheard them talking, but the only thing he could understand was "Hong Kong."

That evening, Detective Po called her colleague, Peter Wong, a detective with the Hong Kong Police Force. He logged on to the airline database to query for Chinese nationals whose flights originated in Miami. Three names appeared on his display. Detective Wong discussed the case with his assistant, Winston Barrister, a British national who was assigned to Hong Kong 25 years ago and never left.

Detective Wong said, "I know one of these guys. He's Tai Lee, a jewel thief who has stolen valuables here and in Singapore. He's very dangerous and also a very skilled race car driver. Let's start with him. He could lead us to the brains behind this caper."

"Winston, put out an all-points bulletin and cross-reference driver's licenses at the expressway booths and the Star Ferry terminal."

Back at the Red Box production facility, Matt, José, and Don Carlos were installing new security systems and procedures. "The more I think about it, the more convinced I am that this was an inside job," José said. "We'll get to the bottom of this."

"I hope so," Matt said. "Now let's head out to Homestead and check on the progress of Baldie 4."

Two days later, Detective Barrister contacted his boss. "We have a match on the Red Box case, a silver Aston Martin pulling out of the airport," he said. "He's 20 minutes away from the Star Ferry."

"Great. Good work," Detective Wong said. "Take the Interceptor and get down to the ferry terminal. Oh, and Barrister, wear your vest."

"Yes, sir," Detective Barrister said. "I know this character, and he's carrying at least one weapon." With sirens blaring, he made it to the terminal in record time. He alerted the Victoria Island police to meet the ferry.

The ferry arrived and Detective Barrister pulled his car onto the boat. He then went to the pilot house and carefully scanned the cars that were coming aboard, looking for the Aston Martin. But when the loading was complete, there was no Aston Martin to be found.

"Something's wrong here," Barrister thought as he called Detective Wong.

"Boss, he's disappeared," he told Wong. The chief detective told Barrister to stay on the ferry and have the Victoria authorities pull all of the trucks over to the inspection lot.

"If he's in one of those trucks, we'll flesh him out," the savvy senior detective said.

Fifteen minutes later, a police team with a canine patrol began searching the commercial vehicles. Detective Barrister took a position by the gate behind the barrier with several police officers.

As the search team approached a low rider delivery truck, the tailgate slammed down and a silver sports car raced to the gate. The driver was firing a handgun and the passenger a submachine gun. One officer was wounded as Detective Barrister hid behind the Interceptor's engine and managed to get a couple shots off, aiming at the tires. The bullets sparked off the pavement as the car, now verified as the Aston Martin, sped away down Des Voeux Road Central onto the Queensway and headed toward the Wan Chai District. At breakneck speed, with Barrister in hot pursuit, the Aston Martin turned onto Hennessy Road leading to the Expressway. The two cars passed Happy Valley Sports Ground at double the posted speed and entered the Aberdeen Tunnel.

They sped down Island Road running to Deep Water Bay. Occasionally each car would get an errant shot at the other along the curvy road toward Repulse Bay. Barrister was within five car lengths when they entered the dangerous South Bay Road toward Stanley, where squad cars had barricaded the road.

Minutes later, the Aston Martin was going too fast for the infamous Tau Chou curve and was launched over the sea cliff. Several explosive fireballs erupted as debris was flung into the waters of Chung Hom Wan bay.

Detective Barrister reported back to Detective Wong, thanked the officers in Stanley, and retraced his harrowing chase back to Hong Kong.

The next day he filed a report and copied Detective Po back in Miami, who then called Matt with the results.

"Chin Chin, we're not at the end of this saga," Matt said.

"I believe you're right, Matt. I'll stay alert for any developments in the case," the detective said.

Matt ended the call by saying, "Thank you for giving up your vacation to help us. I hope to see you soon under different circumstances. Ever been to Belize?"

After a short silence, Chin Chin replied, "Where is that?"

Chapter 10

ROLLOUT

In September the FAA certified the Baldie for flight over American airspace. Matt took the call from Paula in his Miami office with Murray, Maggie, and José hovering over the speakerphone.

"Matt, I think you're going to like our findings and ruling," Paula said. "In short, the Baldie has been certified, with the usual conditions and inspections, for use over U.S. soil. The documents will be couriered to you tomorrow. Congratulations! Your proud bird is now cleared for limited production per the plan submitted last April."

"Paula, you've made our day — indeed, many days to come," Matt replied. "I will notify our team in Belize and our colleagues in Vance. Your efforts are truly appreciated. Please plan to be an honored guest at the rollout in June."

"I gladly accept, and I'm sure the administrator will want to be there as well," Paula said.

"Thanks again, Paula," Matt replied. "We'll talk again soon."

As he hung up the phone, shouts of joy could be heard throughout the facility. Murray shed a tear as he put his arm around Maggie. A huge smile came over José's face.

Matt stood up and said, "I need to make a few phone calls. Maggie, please work with José and Heather to organize a celebratory pig roast at the Homestead hangar on Saturday. I think a few of our German friends will really appreciate it."

"Will do, Matt," Maggie said.

Matt sat down, reflected a minute, and called Reinhold Timm in Vance.

"Reinhold," he said, "We're certified. Please schedule the rollout in June and, if your schedule allows, please come to Miami this weekend for our celebration with a couple of key line supervisors."

"Yes, sir," Timm said. "We'll be there! The chairman will be quite happy."

"Yes, indeed," Matt said. "I'll call Angela now."

As he hung up the phone, he reflected on the four-year journey to get to this moment and how the Baldie would be instrumental in the global acceptance of his brother's invention.

Nine months later, the date of the rollout had arrived. Guests started to arrive in Vance, and the Flynns took separate flights on executive jets provided by Mercedes-Benz. The Baldie team consisted of Matt, Murray, Heather, Maggie, José, Jim, and Aaron.

Mercedes-Benz Chairman von Boltz brought his A team: Chief Engineer Reiner Strassburg, Chief Pilot Horst Neumann, Director of Global Marketing Bernhard Holzmann, and Chief of Security Angela Dicter.

Reinhold Timm, the Vance factory manager, served as the host to a distinguished U.S. Government team consisting of FAA administrator Orin Wright; FAA Project Manager Paula Frankel; DARPA Director George Sebastian; Secretary of Defense Jefferson Palmer; Secretary of the Treasury Adam Aurum; Chief Economist Clayton Feller; President Werner's campaign manager, Bill Cavanaugh; and congressional representatives, including the two senators from Alabama.

Members of the intelligence community were located around the plant along with security and emergency response teams.

On behalf of President Werner, Secretary Aurum was given the honor of christening the production line by cutting the ribbon to open the south doors of the new Baldie Production Facility, or, as the bureaucrats liked to call it, BPF.

Promptly at 11, the large doors parted and Baldie 6 was towed out in front of the grandstand. Engineer Timm welcomed the honored guests and turned the microphone over to Matt, who served as the master of ceremonies. He very carefully introduced all of the important guests.

After 30 minutes of speeches touting the accomplishments to date and the potential global impact of the Baldie, Chief Pilot Horst Neumann, accompanied by Aaron Adams as co-pilot, climbed into the Baldie to prepare for a demonstration flight. With the preflight checklists completed and the Red Box activated, Captain Neumann taxied to the edge of the automobile test track as security helicopters hovered around the plant. The white Baldie gleamed in the bright morning sun. In an instant the 20-ton craft was weightless and hovering 40 feet above the tarmac. The guests watched in amazement behind a cluster of network cameras.

Captain Neumann then made a ceremonial run around the automotive test track, varying the altitude from 5 feet to 11 feet in graceful dives and climbs. Because the Baldie was weightless, the engine thrust was barely audible, comparable to a Mercedes-Benz sports car that might normally occupy the track.

Baldie 6 taxied to within 200 feet of the grandstand, turned around, and instantly rose straight up, as if lifted by a tornado, to an altitude of 800 feet. The guests strained their eyes as Baldie released a water vapor trail against the azure sky. The craft proceeded to complete a series of complex maneuvers typical of an advanced fighter jet at an air show. The stunned audience followed the vapor trail with amazement. The Baldie then suddenly disappeared over the southern horizon just west of the little town of Vance.

Matt took the microphone to assure the audience that everything had gone as planned. Just as he asked the guests not to be alarmed, the Baldie appeared above the plant from the north in stealth mode and slowly descended to the viewing paddock.

With tears in their eyes, the audience burst into applause, as if they had witnessed a Wright brothers flight. A few moments later, the hatch opened and Captain Neumann waved to the cheering crowd before he and co-pilot Adams, who carried the Red Box, proceeded to the production line, where a mass of workers was clapping in the doorway.

The ceremony closed with a video of Chairman von Boltz ushering in a new era of transportation — safe, economical, and a "global game changer," to quote his American friends. He said Mercedes-Benz was proud to have been selected for this honor and was committed to globalizing the Baldie production, including more plants in America.

As the press corps conducted interviews, the Secretary of Defense could be seen surrounded by aides with nodding heads. Paula slipped out of the audience and joined Aaron in the production facility.

Promptly at 12:30, Bavarian cuisine was served in the executive dining room. Matt provided a toast and asked Murray to stand and take a bow. The audience stood up to acknowledge the accomplishment as Maggie hugged Murray in celebration.

Chapter 11

CAMPAIGN

At a cabinet meeting the following week, Secretaries Aurum and Jefferson told President Werner about the rollout. In unison they used the words "awesome" and "game changing." The treasury secretary proclaimed that the $1 billion requested by the Flynns was a bargain for the nation given the potential for new tax revenues from companies and individuals. After the meeting, the president was on the phone to Dallas, talking with his campaign manager, Bill Cavanaugh.

"Bill," he said, "I want the Baldie to be a keystone in my re-election campaign. It's not too late. Call me back in a week with some plans." Cavanaugh, a rotund, jovial dealmaker from Dallas, smiled at the assignment. On his return trip to Dallas from the rollout, Cavanaugh already surmised it would be an important part of the campaign for all the right reasons: jobs, balance of payments, Department of Defense budget, transportation infrastructure, even reigniting the space business — just what Houston needed.

Later that day he summoned his team and showed the video of the Baldie rollout. "President Werner called this morning. He wants to highlight the Baldie in the campaign this summer," he told them. The savvy marketer went over to his desk drawer, pulled out a round, white object, and threw it on the coffee table in front of his staff. It was a 1M lapel button.

"Let's make this happen," he said. "Go brainstorm and come back in two hours."

Two hours later, Cavanaugh reconvened the meeting by saying, "We just got the latest poll numbers. The president's popularity is slipping. We need Baldie now more than ever. Your ideas have got to be good."

His senior staff director called up a document on his laptop. "Bill, we have several ideas that should work," he said as he pointed to a list of items projected from his computer onto a screen in the conference room:

- "1M" media blitz with commercials showing the president taking credit for a job creation initiative
- Visit by President Werner to Vance, Alabama, for a media event
- Weekly briefings by the vice president to members of Congress about the Baldie's impact on home districts
- Digital billboards in swing cities that show the Baldie in flight
- Squads of young women for Baldie (aka "Baldiettes") handing out literature at conventions, key sporting events, and county and state fairs
- Talk show interviews of cabinet members extolling the virtues of the Baldie
- A "60 Minutes" segment on the program
- A website with application contests with rewards, including Baldie rides in Belize
- Creation of "Scientists for Baldie," a nonprofit organization highlighting this enviro-friendly tool on the ground, in the sky, and even in space
- A Baldie Magic online game that would allow players to virtually fly a Baldie around the world
- Creation of Veterans for Baldie, with incentives for veterans organizations singing the praises of the new job creator
- Baldie corndogs for fairs and stadiums
- Baldie ice cream bar for national consumption
- Baldie-shaped pasta

Cavanaugh spoke up: "Guys, these are really good. Drop the food ideas and work up a budget. I want to brief the chief on Monday."

The team adjourned to a cigar bar. A staffer suggested a Baldie cigar label in jest. Cavanaugh shouted across the table, "No Baldie's going to go up in smoke on my watch!"

Chapter 12

CAMP DAVID

Two weeks later, Rita Morales called Matt to invite him to Camp David in June.

"Matt, President Werner wants to discuss Baldie's role during the re-election campaign," Rita said.

It was a pretty easy decision. "Sure," Matt said. "There will be four of us. Murray needs to stay here to start up a new Red Box production line."

"Perfect. I look forward to seeing you again," Rita said. "Give my best to José. Goodbye."

Early in June Baldie 4 flew from Miami northward along the Atlantic coastline. Just north of Norfolk over the Chesapeake Bay, Baldie flew through an early summer squall and was hit by lightning several times.

"Let's land at the marina in Deale, Maryland, and check for damage," Captain Russell said.

"Deale it is," co-pilot Adams said. The craft splashed down a couple hundred yards from the marina and slowly motored through the no-wake zone to the refueling station. After shaking a lot of hands of curious mariners, Matt climbed back into Baldie 4 for the last leg of the journey to Frederick, Maryland.

Back onboard, Matt told Maggie, "I think they're going to ask us to show Baldie at some key sites around the country to reinforce the 1M strategy. I could be wrong, but that's what I would do if I were president."

Maggie smiled with delight at the prospect.

Twenty minutes later, Baldie 4 landed at the Frederick airport, about 20 miles south of Camp David. Shortly after they landed, a helicopter picked them up for the 10-minute flight over apple orchards and into Catoctin Mountain Park. Aaron Adams carried the Red Box. Rita met them at the heliport and escorted the Baldie team into the living room. Secretary Palmer and Bill Cavanaugh rose from the leather sofas in front of fieldstone fireplace to greet their newfound friends.

They were exchanging stories about the rollout when President Werner strode into the room and greeted his guests.

"Thank you for coming. I'm so glad to see you. Please have a seat," he said as he gestured toward the sofas.

"I'll get right down to business," the president said. He turned to his campaign manager as continued, "Bill here believes your Baldie could be a real crowd pleaser during my re-election campaign. It's not enough to have videos on TV. We need a barnstorming tour in August and September."

"The Baldie is up to the task, Mr. President," Matt said. The Baldie team nodded its approval.

"My staff suggests that you start in July at our national convention in Miami. It will inspire the delegates. Shortly after that you would go to America's largest air show in Oshkosh, Wisconsin, where there's a crowd of aircraft owners who are usually of my political persuasion. Then, in September and October, you would tour across the country, landing in a half-dozen major cities. Secretary Palmer can coordinate this with military air shows and, of course, will provide the necessary security."

"Mr. President, what do you expect Baldie to do?" Matt asked.

"Not too much. A few simple maneuvers in the air — about 10 minutes — and a static display," the president said. "Just its presence will remind the voters who welcomed this technology into our society. And, of course, we'll have a booth with young ladies handing out 1M buttons. We'll pick up all of the expenses. And by the way, Secretary Palmer is working up a new defense budget that has both classified and unclassified line items for the Baldie and the Red Box."

"I like the sound of that, Mr. President," Matt said.

"I thought you would," the president said. He then turned to Captain Russell and said, "Captain, I understand you're a pretty good golfer."

The captain was flattered by the compliment and replied, "Well, sir, I have my good days."

At that point Rita entered the room with a bag of golf clubs.

"Recognize these, Captain?" the president asked.

"They look a lot like mine, sir," Jim said in astonishment.

"They are. They were FedExed here yesterday. We need another player for our foursome. What do you say?"

Jim looked around at his colleagues in amazement.

Matt slapped Jim on the back and said, "What are you waiting for? Enjoy yourself. You've earned it, my friend."

The captain smiled and said, "I'd love to!"

"Great," President Werner said. "Meet me at the heliport in 20 minutes."

"Yes, sir!" the captain said.

The president continued, "Matt, your team will have dinner with us and be our guests overnight. While Jim and I are swinging a club, Secretary Palmer would like to pick your brain about how the Baldie and the Red Box can help our military and national defense forces. We'll convene back here at 5 for happy hour."

The first lady joined the group for cocktails and dinner. Afterward, everyone enjoyed the fire pit, cognac, and cool mountain air. Sleep came easy for the Baldie team. The helicopter returned in the morning, and Baldie 4 had an uneventful flight back to Miami.

Six weeks later, Baldie 4 was floating in a Miami marina between two behemoth cruise ships. Delegates to the party's national convention were bused from the convention center. The guests visited the craft in small, six-person groups. Maggie, Heather, and Aaron took turns providing a 15-minute tour. Guests could see the Red Box but not touch it. Multiple security teams stood watch around the clock. Heather mused, "Imagine a cruise ship in the air!" Maggie chuckled at the thought.

On the last day of the convention, just after President Werner was renominated, Baldie 4 gracefully lifted off the water to the amazement of hundreds of cruise ship passengers, leaning over the railings of their ships. It headed toward the Atlantic Ocean and banked left to begin the trip to Wisconsin.

A few hours later, Captain Russell contacted the control tower at Oshkosh, Wisconsin, for landing instructions. True to their word, Secretary Palmer and Bill Cavanaugh had made all of the arrangements — premier static display location, hospitality chalet, security details, hotel rooms, and, of course, a campaign booth extolling the accomplishments of the Werner administration, including videos of the rollout at Vance.

Promptly at noon each day, Aaron or Maggie would activate the Red Box and Baldie would quickly rise straight above the sea of airplanes. The proud bird would do a figure eight over the main runway, return to the center of the airfield, execute a nose-down bow to the grandstand, and then, as if by magic, ascent vertically out of sight. The crowd screamed its delight. Four minutes later, Baldie 4 appeared at the end of the runway. Thousands of teary eyes watched the almost silent craft assume its static display position as VIPs lifted flutes of champagne in their chalets. On the fourth day, Baldie 4 again lifted off the tarmac, but this time headed west on its way to Seattle's Sea-Tac International Airport.

Matt joined the tour in Seattle in order to personally brief Boeing executives about the Baldie. He viewed Boeing as a logical second source producer in America while Mercedes-Benz expanded its production to Europe and the Far East. The Baldie 4 followed the Oshkosh program in Seattle. However, there was one less show to allow Baldie's visit to the Boeing plant. Seasoned albeit skeptical aeronautical engineers uniformly approved of the revolutionary technology. The next day, company executives assembled a "skunk works" team to develop a production plan and cost and licensing proposals, which were ultimately approved by the Flynns in October. After its last performance in the rain at SEA-TAC, Baldie flew to San Francisco.

During the two-day air shows there, security was increased due to the large Asian population in the Bay Area. There was a photo op over the Golden Gate Bridge. The team also took some time off to tour the area. One stop was the BOAC flying boat at the aviation museum at Oakland International Airport. The craft typically operated out of Miami from the 1930s to the 1950s, serving eight wealthy passengers in the best style of the day. "Boy, have we come a long way!" Maggie mused. "Maybe we should give it a new life with a Red Box." In unison the team members shook their heads and responded with a resounding, "No!"

The next stop on the tour was Marine Corps Base Camp Pendleton, halfway between Los Angeles and San Diego. The air show there was impressive, with jump jets, the Osprey, and attack helicopters. But the Baldie stole the show. Marine generals could see the craft taking leathernecks into combat. Political booths were not allowed, so large billboards showing President Werner with a faint Baldie in the background were strategically placed along California Highway 5. The secretary of defense made a surprise visit, much to the delight of the Marines. Baldie 4 showed no signs of wear when Captain Russell did his preflight walkaround. After the hatch closed, Maggie activated the Red Box, and soon the eagle logo could be seen over Barstow, California, on its way to Chicago.

On Lake Michigan, Baldie floated majestically at the end of Navy Pier — just in time for the American Legion's annual convention with its 15,000 Legionnaires. By this time, Heather and Maggie were practically celebrities due to the tour's ongoing media coverage. President Werner gave the keynote address to a very supportive audience. Matt glowed in the spotlight and often wished Murray were with him to enjoy the experience.

The president's plan was working; Baldie was given some credit for the rise in his approval ratings.

The next stop could have been predicted by anyone following the tour: the Big Apple.

On a sunny September day, Matt accepted the Key to the City as Baldie 4 floated at the ferry terminal at the lower end of Manhattan. During this three-day stop, half a day was orchestrated as a photo op with flyovers at the Statue of Liberty. Crowds lined the Hudson River to watch Baldie glide effortlessly up and down the river. The show was repeated on the East River, where diplomats could watch from the windows of the United Nations. Murray called Matt to inform him that the new production line was operational.

On their last night in New York, the Baldie team enjoyed dinner and schmoozing with celebrities atop the Trump Tower. "The Donald" told reporters he would buy the first unit off the production line in Vance. Matt didn't tell him he had dozens of requests for the same thing in his desk at the Miami facility.

Early the next day, the Baldie rose above the ferry terminal, turned southwest, and flew over New Jersey toward its last stop on the tour: Houston.

After circumnavigating several thunderstorms in east Texas, Baldie 4 landed at Houston's Hobby Airport. This was an important stop because two days prior President Werner had made a campaign speech at the nearby Johnson Space Center, where he hinted that "someday the Red Box could rekindle the space industry and create thousands of jobs."

Thousands of 1M buttons were handed out. Another photo op saw Baldie fly by the display of the Saturn V — the rocket that took Americans to the moon. Bill Cavanaugh proclaimed the visit to be an absolute success. After accepting another Key to the City, Matt turned to Captain Russell and said, "Head home, my friend."

Three hours later, Baldie 4 landed at the Homestead airport. José ran to greet it. As Matt stepped out of the craft, José handed him a confirmation statement from Belize, which confirmed the deposit of the first half of the $1 billion promised by the U.S. Government.

Chapter 13

ROSE BOWL

A month after the Camp David meeting, Baldie 4 flew to Los Angeles. Captain Russell taxied the craft to the business jet service tarmac, where it was immediately met by one of Secretary Palmer's security details. Maggie served as the co-pilot and guarded the Red Box. Matt, Jim, and Maggie were met by the Mercedes-Benz marketing director, Bernhard Holzmann. "Welcome to LAX," he said. "I have a car that will take us to the Hilton near the airport entrance."

On the way to the hotel, Holzmann told the team, "This year the Super Bowl will be held at the Rose Bowl in Pasadena. Mercedes-Benz is a major sponsor. It is my job to have the Baldie somehow associated with the halftime show. Needless to say, Matt, your suggestion of Baldie delivering the band has generated a lot of interest. I mean A LOT of interest."

Matt wasn't promising anything novel or risky for Baldie. He was in Los Angeles to convince the organizing committee that this dramatic event was not only possible, but also inherently safe.

At lunch the team reviewed its briefing, complete with video testimonials and flight footage. At 2 p.m. Holzmann led the committee members into the Concorde Conference Room. The committee included NFL

Commissioner Tyrone Dobbs, a former player for the Chicago Bears; Marty McGuire, Super Bowl organizer; Cheryl Clark, the halftime event manager; and Harvey Rubinstein, manager of the Rose Bowl security office. Each was accompanied by two or three staff members.

After introductions, Matt stepped to the podium and introduced his chief pilot. Jim Russell then narrated two videos of the Baldie in flight, emphasizing its safety features. Maggie placed a Red Box in the center of the conference table. It seemed to mesmerize the audience.

Matt returned to the podium and showed a video of the rollout in Vance. He detailed the certification process and the safety procedures that required FAA approval. He then presented a 3-D simulation of Baldie 5 coming over the north wall of the Rose Bowl and dropping down to the football field. Five figures came of the hatch, representing the band members. Baldie then made one circle around the field before shooting straight up.

The committee asked a lot of questions, each answered with alacrity by Matt and Jim. Holzmann assured the audience that Mercedes-Benz produces only safe vehicles, even if they can fly. This was the lead-in for Matt to invite the committee to be passengers on Baldie the next morning on the north runway at LAX. They accepted.

At 7:30 a.m. the following day, two limousines pulled up next to the Baldie and Matt welcomed eight committee members at the hatch. The Baldie was outfitted like an expensive business jet, with plush leather chairs. Each committee member had a window seat.

Maggie activated the Red Box and Captain Russell taxied west to the end of the runway where it meets the Pacific Ocean. The craft rose straight up, and at 1,000 feet headed west. Ten minutes later the Baldie was circling Catalina Island. The flight plan allowed it to land on a high school football field in a dress rehearsal for the Super Bowl. Matt reinforced the safety features on the return trip. After landing, the committee members each shook Matt's hand. The last to do so was NFL Commissioner Dobbs, who said, "This was fantastic. I'll have a decision for you in a month. We have a lot to think about."

Four weeks later to the day, the commissioner called Matt. "Mr. Flynn, you've got a winner," he said. "It's a go for Baldie, and I've reserved four seats in my booth for your team. I hope this meets with your approval."

"It certainly does," an excited Matt said. "And you should know that there will only be four band members. The drummer doesn't like to fly and will be prestaged on the ground." They both chuckled. Matt thanked the commissioner and hung up the phone. He then called Holzmann with the good news. He asked him if Chairman von Boltz would like to attend the game with him.

"Matt, you're a genius," Holzmann replied. "You should have my job, too!"

"No thanks, Bernhard," Matt said. "I've got plenty to do right here. Auf Wiedersehen."

Chapter 14

LANDSLIDE

In late October Matt and Heather were lounging by the pool when the phone rang.

"Hi, Heather," Bill Cavanaugh said. "Is Matt there?" She handed the cell phone to Matt.

"Hi, Bill. What's up?"

"Matt, on behalf of President Werner, I'd like to invite you and Heather to the campaign headquarters to watch the election returns on November 6. I'd invite Murray and Maggie, but I have a feeling that they are apolitical."

"You're right about that, Bill," Matt replied. He asked Heather if she wanted to attend. She nodded her approval and Matt said, "Bill, we'd be delighted to attend."

"Great. I've booked a room at the Willard. You know where it is. See you soon, Matt."

//\\

As the couple arrived in the hotel's ornate, gilded lobby on the morning of Election Day, they were greeted by Rita Morales. "So glad you could make it," she said. "Bill's convinced your invention and the barnstorming tour made a big difference. Here are your 1M buttons." As she escorted the Flynns to the elevator, she continued, "Jobs, more jobs, and high-paying jobs will be the theme of tonight's speeches."

As Matt and Heather settled into their room, Matt through back to the last time he was at the hotel. It was in March, when the team was preparing to brief the president. A lot had happened since then, he thought to himself.

The couple spent the day at the National Gallery of Art and the Newseum, then returned to the hotel to treat themselves to a spa package. They joined friends for happy hour at the lobby bar, where the conversation revolved around politics and the unfolding election. Much to Heather's dismay, the bartender had never heard of a Baldie cocktail. Matt sipped his Manhattan and said to his wife, "The president's going to win by a large margin because the opposition is promising the wrong kind of jobs. They are only promising bureaucratic jobs here in Washington to manage the ever-growing welfare state."

Heather quickly changed the subject, asking, "Do you think Baldie 6 will be ready by January?"

Matt answered, "Yes, he will be. All reports from Belize are positive, and the weather is cooperating to allow us to meet the test schedule."

His face then lit up as an idea came to him. "Say, what do you think about spending Christmas in San Pedro" he asked his wife. "It's just as easy to decorate a palm tree there as it is in Key Biscayne."

Heather thought for a moment, then responded, "I like the idea. And let's invite José and Don Carlos and their families. They deserve a vacation."

"Great idea, honey. I'll invite them tomorrow."

An hour later they were seated at Bill Cavanaugh's table in the main dining room. Small talk eased the tension of the occasion. During dessert, Bill rose, clinked his glass to request silence, and delivered a very gracious toast to the Flynns, who were asked to stand and be recognized. The applause caused Heather to blush ever so slightly. As Matt looked at her he was reminded of Eric Clapton's song, "Wonderful Tonight." He smiled contentedly as several $100,000 club members slapped him on the back and shook his hand. A tall Texan asked, "When can I get a ride on Baldie?" Matt promptly replied, "Any day down in Belize, which is only a two-hour plane ride from Houston."

"I just might do that!" the Texan replied. They laughed together.

By 10 p.m. the main ballroom was filling up as election returns and newscasts were displayed on large monitors that ringed the room. Early projections supported Matt's prediction. The Flynns were introduced to a lot of wealthy couples and found themselves enjoying the limelight. Matt thought to himself, "I wonder if any of these folks would like to invest in the next application of the Red Box."

By midnight the landslide was apparent. The challenger was only going to win Massachusetts, Oregon, and the District of Columbia. At 12:30, President Werner entered the ballroom and thanked his supporters in a short but sincere speech. As he left the room, he spotted the Flynns and came over to them and shook their hands as he said, "We'll see you two again real soon." He quickly disappeared behind a phalanx of Secret Service agents.

Matt and Heather retired to their room and changed into flannel pajamas to ward off a cold, rainy night. As they snuggled in bed, Matt asked, "Honey, what do you think the next application of the Red Box should be?"

Heather was quick to answer. "I don't know, Matt, but I'll give it some thought."

They kissed goodnight and fell asleep in each other's arms.

Chapter 15

SUPER BOWL

Two weeks after President Werner's inauguration, two teams who had never played in the Super Bowl were at the Rose Bowl, attempting to win the biggest prize in American football. Baldie 6 had flown in the night before the game and was housed in a temporary canvas shelter erected in a parking lot just north of the stadium. The shelter was the idea of Rose Bowl Security Director Harvey Rubinstein, who felt it would provide security for the aircraft and privacy for the band members. Maggie helped Jim and Adam with the preflight checklist that afternoon. She later joined Matt, Chairman von Boltz, and Bernhard Holzmann in the commissioner's booth.

Midway through the second quarter, a limousine dropped four band members off at the shelter. Captain Russell did a final walk-around inspection and gave the thumbs-up to his co-pilot. He secured the hatch and walked up to the cockpit.

A few minutes before halftime, security gave the all-clear signal and the tent covering Baldie was rolled back. A short time later, the first half ended in a close game. As the teams left the field, a sea of stagehands erected a platform on which the band would perform and the Baldie was cleared for takeoff. Adam activated the Red Box and Baldie 6, already pointed toward the Rose Bowl, rose with no effort and very little sound to an altitude of 100 feet as the captain edged the craft toward the north wall of the stadium. With the band members peering out the windows, Baldie suddenly appeared like an alien spaceship about 80 feet above the stunned crowd. Matt smiled as he thought of Murray watching it on television with tears in his eyes.

Baldie's shadow passed over part of the crowd as Captain Russell positioned the craft over the platform. Baldie 6 looked bigger than life on the Jumbotron as it landed gently on the field. The public address announcer welcomed the Baldie and introduced the band as they left the port hatch and took up their instruments. The applause was deafening as the band opened with a few bars of the theme from "Star Trek." Co-pilot Adams closed the hatch and returned to the cockpit. Captain Russell then raised the proud bird straight up to an altitude of 300 feet before he activated a water vapor trail. Laser lights emanated from both sides of Baldie 6. Captain Russell told his co-pilot, "Here we go!" and an instant later, Baldie, although perfectly level with the ground, shot straight up in its now famous flying saucer maneuver.

In the Security Operations Center, Harvey Rubinstein's team did a round of high fives.

In the parking lot, huge Mercedes-Benz trucks pulled up to the gate entrances and unloaded Baldie T-shirts and memorabilia of all shapes and sizes.

Network and cable news channels ran footage of the event from several different angles. Across America, people who had never sent a text message grabbed their cell phones and tried to do so.

And in the NFL commissioner's box, Dobbs shook hands with Matt and Chairman von Boltz, saying, "Congratulations, gentlemen. You've created a once-in-a-lifetime occasion never to be forgotten."

Maggie called Murray and handed the cell phone to Matt. With tears in his eyes, Matt told Murray, "You did it, brother. You did it!" Holzmann was on the phone with Reinhold Timm, the factory manager in Vance, where a huge Super Bowl party was underway in the employee cafeteria.

A minute later, Maggie got a call from Aaron, stating that the Baldie had landed safely at LAX. He could hardly believe the event was over as he packed the Red Box in his backpack and gleefully took a call from Paula.

That evening, Chairman von Boltz hosted a dinner at a swank restaurant in Marina del Rey. There were two questions on the chairman's mind: How could this spectacular event ever be topped? And what's the next application of the Red Box? He was particularly interested in Matt's response to the second question.

"I don't know, sir," Matt replied. "But later this week we are having a meeting in Belize to discuss it, and hopefully we'll answer that question. I hope some of the members of your team will join us."

"Of course," von Boltz said. "At a minimum, I will send Bernhard, Reiner, Reinhold, and Angela."

"Perfect," Matt said. "That will give a perspective from sales, engineering, production, and security."

As the team left the restaurant they got a congratulatory call from President Werner. Before ending the call, he told them, "We've just wired something to your bank in Belize."

Everyone knew what he meant.

Chapter 16

THE VOTE

The overnight flight from Pasadena to Ambergris Caye benefited from a strong tailwind and a mood of quiet joy. The reality of the new technology really sunk in for the team when the Baldie appeared over the Rose Bowl wall. It was a once-in-a-lifetime experience for the 100,000 people who witnessed it in person. As the proud bird touched down at the airport in Belize, Matt told the team to get some sleep because they would need all the energy they could muster for think tank sessions to determine the next application for the Red Box and for a well-deserved, weeklong celebration of their achievements.

Murray arrived the next morning via commercial flight and water taxied to Ambergris Caye. He was in extremely high spirits from the Rose Bowl success, which legitimized his invention. He was ready to do it again in another application that could impact the lives of billions of people.

After a leisurely breakfast by the Sunbreeze hotel pool, the 11-person party took their coffee into the conference veranda overlooking the Gulf. Seated around the table were the four Flynns — Matt, Murray, Heather, and Maggie — along with Captain Russell, Paula Frankel (who was now engaged to Aaron Adams), and three Mercedes-Benz principals hand-picked by the CEO: Reiner Strassburg, Bernhard Holzmann, and

Reinhold Timm. John Baldinger served as the secretary, keeping minutes and providing the occasional comment about the patentability of a given idea, while Angela Dicter contributed her security expertise.

From his seat at the end of the table, Matt recalled the steps that had brought them to this occasion. "With a little bit of genius and luck, along with a lot of hard work and a few harrowing moments, we prevailed. We have the product, the protection, the exposure, and the financial backing from both the good ol' USA and our friends from Mercedes-Benz. So now is the time to plan for the next chapter in this world-altering adventure while the plant in Vance produces the next increment of Baldies.

"We're going to discuss the follow-on application each morning for three days, followed by fun each afternoon and a banquet each night. Today, I'm going to expose you to the nine applications my brother and I feel are worthy of discussion. Tomorrow we will debate the merits of each, and on Friday we'll take a vote and lay out a preliminary development plan. We will assign engineering, marketing, and balance sheet tasks and reconvene in a month to finalize the plan. Any objections, questions, or comments?"

Silence filled the room.

"Good. Let's get started," Matt said. "Let me start by saying that the Treasury check didn't bounce and the Caye International Bank now has over a billion dollars in our account."

Laughter and applause erupted from the group.

"And please keep in mind the model in the USA works, so we will license industries for production with national government backing by country and in some cases by region."

Matt, Murray, and Jim led the discussion that followed. Maggie put up the first slide as an agenda. It listed the following applications:

- Commercial aviation
- Military

- The marine industry
- Space
- Agriculture
- The construction industry
- Theme parks
- Mercedes-Benz products already in production
- The Personal Baldie

Captain Russell described how the Red Box would revolutionize commercial aviation. "The Red Box enables new designs that do not have to depend upon airfoil lift," he explained. "These are designs that are inherently safe and do not fall from the sky. With dramatically smaller engines, the fuel savings are enormous, not to mention the cost of pollution around airports. Long runways are no longer required and the aircraft can be much larger, accommodating more passengers at a reduced fare. It's a win-win scenario, if you ask me." Captain Russell detailed many other advantages before pointing to his two Mercedes-Benz cohorts and saying, "Plus, it puts Mercedes-Benz in the airplane business. I rest my case."

Matt interjected, "Remember, the discussion/debate is tomorrow."

Murray then stood up and gave a detailed description of the ways the Red Box could be applied to the military. "Think about it," he told his rapt audience. "We can change the very nature of warfare. The old rules no longer apply. Why? Because all platforms and combatants can fly! This will change the very tactics we rely upon. Marine squads will fly to the enemy in stealth, shielded from radar by natural terrain, only to surprise — day or night — with a lethal force. Imagine an aircraft carrier that does not require water to travel to the fight. Army convoys would move silently in flight — much faster and with no threat of the dreaded IEDs. Here, too, the fuel savings alone would keep money in the Treasury, and that money could be used to buy more talent or benefit our troops."

Matt took over the discussion by turning to the marine industry. "New cruise ships would be more economical to operate and inherently unsinkable. The ship lands at a dock for port visits. It would eliminate the need for canals and lochs and associated fees. Special routes and altitudes would be established so as not to interfere with regular air traffic. Seasickness would be a thing of the past. The application to yachts and pleasure boats of all kinds, even Ski-Doos, would revolutionize the industry and create new jobs around the world."

Murray, always the forward thinker, envisioned a rejuvenated space business. "Rockets could finally leave Earth on deep space missions. In effect, the Space Shuttle would be reincarnated, able to go to Mars. New classes of satellites would be invented. Successful laboratories could be orbited, creating new products like perfect ball bearings for Mercedes-Benz engines. The space race would be rekindled, creating jobs around the planet."

Matt asked, "How about agriculture?"

He answered his own question, saying, "Farming would not be restricted to terra firma. Farms could be floating islands over oceans or deserts. Moving above bad weather when necessary, with plenty of sunlight and no pests or disease. Hydroponics could become an economic boom. Every farm vehicle would save money on fuel. The world's food supply would be increased, driving down the cost and enabling us to feed the malnourished. Oh, and if you wanted to grow pot, you could do that, too!"

"One of my favorite applications is to the construction industry," Murray said. "Why? Without the weight problem, new assembly techniques would be perfected. The national highway, bridge, and rail infrastructure would be modernized at a fraction of today's cost and schedule. There would be no steel beams to fall on people; indeed, every project would be much safer. Shipbuilding would be revolutionized. One of the first subapplications could be the construction of standard, multifunction Baldie terminals in major cities."

The audience quickly grasped the national and global impacts of the application.

"And, let's not forget the entertainment business," Matt said. "Can you imagine today's athletes being weightless? The games would be changed forever, even the Olympics. Cowboys could ride weightless bulls. NASCAR races would be on an oval 200 feet above the fans. And what about theme parks? Remember the pleasure of being weightless? Can you imagine flying roller coasters? Bands would float above the audience. The list for entertainment is long, and it would not take long to put it in place. There's a big business for the Red Box here!"

Reiner Strassburg stood up and described the possible applications to Mercedes-Benz's current line of vehicles. "This would be the easiest to do and bring in the most immediate revenue," he said. "We would apply it to our cars, trucks, and buses immediately — if, and it's a big if, national authorities would adopt regulation to safely control these zero-gravity vehicles. It would be a challenge, of course, to cross national borders without international regulation.

"We would also create new engines and transmissions to mirror the efficiencies gained by the Red Box. As an engineer, I'm excited, indeed thrilled, by the prospect of such an application. We have plants around the world that could be converted for these purposes. I'm not a politician, but I can see many policy implications and what you Americans call 'sandboxes' coming into play here, all adding to very lengthy approval cycles both at the national and global levels."

"Herr Doktor Strassburg," Matt stated, "your corporate support and realism continues to impress me. Thank you!"

"Now I have one more for your consideration," Matt continued. "Simply put, it's the Personal Baldie. You saw the Rose Bowl audience. They were awe-struck. And when it landed and the band members came out, the audience *all* saw themselves as one of them. You see, it's simple: Man wants to fly! Unlike Yves Rossy and his rocket pack, which is spectacular, men and women want to fly in comfort — warm and dry and safe — perhaps with the attention span required for an automobile and not a race car. The personal Baldie would be a two- or four-seater. It could be economically produced using industrial resins via 3-D printers. It would be airtight, if needed, and watertight — sort of like an enclosed Ski-Doo. It would not have to be overpowered to be a hoot to fly. It would have wheels for use on the highway and would change commuter patterns around the country. It could be started as a recreational vehicle used in remote areas while authorities figure out how to handle millions of them in urban areas. Smart people would start by applying the commercial aircraft model for spacing, altitudes, schedules, and the like to accommodate safe traffic. It wouldn't be easy, but it would be possible with international handoff and control procedures in place.

"Personally, I like this application very much because of the inherent need to fulfill man's desire to fly and the relatively low cost of entry. Trials would pressure politicians who, in turn, would pressure bureaucrats to devise workable schemes which could be implemented expeditiously, say in three years or less, without a costly overhaul to the national highway and airway infrastructure.

"And, of course, each Personal Baldie would have a tamper-proof Red Box with an altitude governor. I don't want junior floating up into the stratosphere!"

His comment drew a round of laughter from the team.

"Much like drones, an altitude limit could be set, say at 500 feet, so as not to interfere with air traffic. And let's face it — 500 feet is as high as a 50-story building. You can do a lot and have a lot of fun in this airspace. Wouldn't you each want to have one? Your children certainly would"

He then concluded, "I ask you to seriously think about these potential applications. There may be other uses, but this is enough for today. Now let's adjourn to the bar. The Baldies are on me!"

The next day the meeting started just after breakfast. The morning sun shone brightly through the shuttered veranda room. John Baldinger handed out his summary minutes of the previous day's presentations, which Matt had approved prior to retiring for the evening.

Matt started the meeting by thanking everyone for not discussing the subject at the bar. He said he was eager to have a frank discussion about the alternatives.

"Nobody is to sugar-coat their feelings," he said. "You are here to be blunt because, in the end, billions of dollars are at stake. Please don't discuss these matters over the phone. As you know, we've already had episodes with the Chinese. Their economy needs this technology to create jobs and enable military dominance in the Far East. Need I say more? A lot — a very lot — is at stake here. Voice your observations with clarity and conviction."

The team nodded in agreement.

Matt turned to Baldinger and said, "First, let me ask our legal expert: Which application is in his opinion the easiest to patent?"

Baldinger stood up and said, "In my judgment, a specific Personal Baldie would be the easiest. All of the other application areas can go in so many directions, spawning hundreds of patents, too many to imagine and accomplish in the short term, less than two years. The construction industry alone is ripe for hundreds of different applications and corresponding patents by industry, many of which will be fought by labor unions because the time on the job will be dramatically reduced. Hence, my answer is the Personal Baldie."

Matt thanked his colleague and said, "Next, let me ask Paula and Jim, are the challenges for the aircraft industry insurmountable?"

Jim responded, "Based upon my experience with Baldie, any pilot in the world would love to be in the cockpit. I believe both Aaron and Maggie would support me on this." The two pilots nodded their heads vigorously.

Paula stood up and addressed the group. "I believe we have enough regulations, procedures, and technologies — proven over billions of safe flight miles — that the commercial fight application would ultimately fly."

Murmurs of approval were heard throughout the room.

"OK. Thanks," Matt said. "Now let me turn to our distinguished German guests. Reiner, you mentioned the difficulty of getting your current vehicles approved for flight, nation by nation. Is this still your opinion?"

"Yes. As important as Mercedes-Benz is to national economies, politicians have the last say and, therefore, the approval process will drag on for years. It's tragic but true."

"What about the 3-D manufacturing process I mentioned for the Personal Baldie?" Matt asked. "Is it realistic? Could Mercedes-Benz lead this effort?"

"Yes on both counts," Strassburg answered.

"Mr. Holzmann, may I ask you if there are unforeseen obstacles to marketing a Personal Baldie made by Mercedes-Benz?" Matt asked.

Holzmann immediately responded, "Nichts, nada, no. None that I can see. I believe we could conduct a very powerful campaign, putting a Baldie in every garage!"

"Thank you," Matt said. "Now let's open the discussion. Who's first?"

John Baldinger spoke up. "I, for one, would like to hear what Heather has to say. She's been with the project from the beginning."

"Of course," Matt said. "Heather, what's your view?"

She paused for a moment, then said, "This is a business decision that must be right the first time. I believe we need to focus on the application or applications which have three major features: easiest to do, greatest visibility, and fewest bureaucratic hurdles. Having said that, I believe the space business would be the easiest to implement. The infrastructure is already in place. The biggest hurdle is fighting gravity, and the Red Box solves that problem. Weightless heavy-lift vehicles would give NASA the capability it sorely needs. Plus, we can easily duplicate the personnel numbers of the moon program, which engaged tens of thousands of companies and employed more than 1 million people. Congress would buy into the program, as would the bureaucrats, because it's a win-win scenario. So I would put the space application right up at the top of the list."

"Sound logic, my dear!" Matt said.

"But wait. I'm not finished."

"Please continue."

"I believe we could accomplish two applications simultaneously. The other is the Personal Baldie. At the same time we put a Red Box in the hands of the engineers at NASA, we could be working with Mercedes-Benz, and perhaps other vehicle manufacturers, to prototype the Personal Baldie. Early prototypes could be used to gain public acceptance while we undertake the Government's certification process. Indeed, we have a test track right here in Ambergris Caye with an airport only four blocks from here, and we could use the one in Vance, Alabama, as well."

"Heather, that's a great way to start our discussion," Matt said as those around the table nodded in agreement.

For the rest of the day, including the lunch break, the room buzzed with an interactive discussion, at times animated and boisterous, as team members began to prioritize the potential applications. The Personal Baldie was gaining favor, while the entertainment business was clearly the lowest priority. In many venues — NASCAR, for example — the liability and insurance would be extremely difficult to overcome.

Promptly at 5 p.m., Matt ended the meeting with a warning not to talk to anyone about the Baldie applications.

"Indeed, let's not talk about the Baldie anymore, but drink one at the bar," he said.

Day Three arrived with a sudden rain shower. The guests quickly retreated to the cover of the veranda for the critical vote session and subsequent planning that would, in many ways, dramatically impact the national and international economy.

John Baldinger passed out a ballot sheet with all of the applications listed. "Take your time," he said. "Reflect on your choices. Mark them one through nine in the priority you believe is the direction this enterprise should take. Return your ballot by 10. Two of us will tally the results and announce them at a working lunch on the beach."

Once the server had cleared the dishes, Matt clinked his glass and reported the results of the vote.

"It should be no surprise to anyone that the Personal Baldie is number one, followed by a tie for number two between the space business and the construction business, largely because of their ability to create jobs," Matt said. "The Personal Baldie is viewed as a trailblazer that would test the markets and run the gauntlet of bureaucratic obstacles to its certification in the American airspace. The Personal Baldie would also be a demonstration for both military and commercial aviation uses. Lower on the list were the marine and agriculture industries. To no one's surprise, the entertainment industry was a solid number nine."

Murray mused, "We looked at this from an American perspective. I wonder what the ranking would be in Germany or China or elsewhere?"

"Good question, Murray," Paula replied. "You know other governments have ways of cutting through the regulations and red tape to promote programs of national interest."

Matt restarted the discussion, saying, "OK. We have our result. Thanks to everyone. So now let's focus on the first steps of a plan to make the Personal Baldie a reality. Murray, are there some early engineering steps we need to take?"

"No, I don't think so," Murray replied. "The Red Box works the same for any platform. What we will have to do is develop a mass production plan to lower the cost, not the quality, to ensure market acceptance. We will quickly outgrow the Miami facility."

"Yes," Matt said. "Perhaps our first task is to commission a design team. Reiner, is this something that Mercedes-Benz could take on?"

"Yes, of course," Strassburg said. "We could support a design team in Alabama."

"Perfect. I'll work out a schedule and budget with you in the near future," Matt said. "Murray, would you and Maggie and Paula develop a briefing we could give to the NASA officials to start the decision process?"

"Sure. That's realistic within a month" Murray replied.

"John, you need to start thinking about the use of the Red Box in the rocket and space business. And once we approve the Personal Baldie design, we will need both an application and a design patent in the U.S. and Europe."

"Matt, the wheels are already in motion," the attorney replied.

"Good. Thanks. Maggie, this project is going to get very complex very soon. I want you to work with Angela to survey each of our locations and install the equipment and procedures to protect every aspect of this endeavor. It's a big task. Are you up to it?"

"Absolutely!"

"I also want you to be one of the test pilots along with Aaron for the Personal Baldie. It will be a hoot, but there is some danger."

"I thought you'd never ask," Maggie said. She noticed Captain Russell wink at her from across the table.

"Reiner, back to you again," Matt said. "I need you to establish a mass production team to work with our Miami crew to get the most Red Box production out of that facility and the secret backup facility. In the process you'll be creating a model for production in multiple remote locations, even Vance."

Reiner replied, "When you mentioned mass production, a light bulb lit up — that is the American expression, correct? I have ideas already."

"Excellent! I knew I could count on you and your teams."

Turning his attention to Mercedes-Benz's global sales executive, Matt said, "Bernhard, you need to be thinking about trade shows where we introduce the Personal Baldie. It could be car shows, but also the Paris Air Show and elsewhere around the globe. Please put a schedule together for my approval. And you also need to think of Murray as an invaluable salesman. Work out a schedule with him where his presence will wow the audiences, but don't wear his butt out going around the globe."

Laughter erupted from the group.

"I'm on it, boss!" Holzmann said.

"Hey, guys, I think that's enough action items for one day," Matt said. "Let's go poolside."

That evening Heather hosted a banquet dinner on the beach under a big tent, complete with an open bar and musicians. A good time was had by all.

Baldie 6 was moored along the pier. Murray and Maggie carried champagne glasses down the pier to be sure the craft was secure. They clinked glasses, kissed, and Maggie said, "You go rejoin the party. I'll lock up here. I'll only be a couple of minutes."

As she checked the lines, she thought for a second she saw frogmen-type shadows under the pier. But she dismissed it, attributing it to her always overactive imagination and that second glass of champagne.

She hummed a happy tune as she made her way back to the party.

THE END

Appendix

CHARACTER DESCRIPTIONS

Matt Flynn
Principal, entrepreneur, businessman, always dreamed of flying like a bird
Age 56
Married to Heather
Medium build, good athlete in college
Very strong face, brown eyes
Good salesman; presenter
Similar to: Burt Lancaster

Murray Flynn
Principal, physicist, inventor of the Red Box
Age 53
Younger brother of Matt, married to Maggie
Always focused
Astronomical math IQ; sometimes too bright
Needs Maggie's common sense
Similar to: Robert Oppenheimer

Heather Flynn

Aeronautical engineer
Age 54, but looks 40
Married to Matt
Tall, slender, red hair, freckles; could be a movie star
Very inquisitive; always asks, "Why?"
Excellent writer; FAA documents
Helped design the Red Box
Similar to: Cintia Dicker, Brazilian model

Maggie Flynn

Pilot, skilled in martial arts
Age 49
Married to Murray
Slender, athletic body
Dark hair and eyes, almost Asian
Murray's alter ego
Works well with Captain Russell
Similar to: Maggie Q

Jim Russell

Chief pilot, flew 747s
Age 55
Detail oriented but able to laugh
Patient; good explainer
Helped train co-pilots Aaron and Maggie
Similar to: Harrison Ford

Aaron Adams

Co-pilot; U.S. Marine Corps jet fighter pilot, executive jet pilot for 14 years
Age 49
Made suggestions during the construction of Baldie 1
5'9", stocky, strong, energetic
Similar to: Matt Damon

José Flores

Sunbreeze Hotel manager
Age 60
Fifth-generation Honduran; claims to have Mayan ancestry (no proof)
Tall, dark complexion, mustache
Loves cigars
Runs a tight ship, including the bar
Similar to: Cesar Romero

Chin Chin Po

Chinese detective based in Hong Kong
Age 44
5'8", strikingly beautiful, delicate features, narrow face, looks more Western than Eastern
Department chief, solves crimes
Similar to: Li Bingbing

Tinshin Wei

Chinese detective based in Hong Kong
Age 34
5'4", very delicate, pretty face
Excellent criminology background
Deputy to Chief Po
Similar to: Ziyi Zhang

José Diaz

Baldie factory manager in Miami
Age 58
UCLA production engineer
No-nonsense leader; loved by employees
Always built airplanes, private pilot
Wants to visit relatives in Cuba
Similar to: Ricardo Montalbán

Don Carlos Fuentes

Baldie Red Box factory assistant manager in Miami
Age 50
Aeronautical engineer turned manager
Similar to: Disarming like Errol Flynn, Orland Bloom; "dashing"

James Cox

Emergency physician at South Miami Hospital
Age 58
Two tours as a Navy doctor aboard ship, former department head at Georgetown University Hospital
Avid tennis player (two replaced knees)
Great bedside manner
Similar to: Sean Connery with a Florida tan

Werner von Boltz

Chairman, Mercedes-Benz, Stuttgart; rose through the ranks
Age 60
Attended the Max Planck Institute for Geophysics at Heidelberg University
Private pilot
Similar to: Wernher von Braun

Reiner Strassburg

Chief engineer, Mercedes-Benz, Stuttgart
Age 62
Considered a styling genius
Held multiple factory leadership positions during 40-year career
Credited with several automotive inventions
Similar to: Young Konrad Adenauer

Reinhold Timm

Factory manager, Mercedes-Benz, Vance, Alabama
Age 55
Knows everything about vehicle manufacturing
Stern but fair; honest and respected by peers
Considers Mercedes-Benz crew family
Avid bass fisherman
Similar to: John Glenn

Bernhard Holzmann

Global Sales Executive, Mercedes-Benz, Stuttgart; Reports to von Boltz, leading company salesman
Age 50
Former Formula 1 racer turned executive
Loves anything fast, knows Mercedes-Benz products
Dashing bachelor, world traveler, comfortable in any environment
Similar to: Golfer Bernhard Langer

Horst Neumann

Chief Pilot, Mercedes-Benz, Stuttgart
Age 51
Executive jet pilot for 25 years
Cool under any circumstance
Always dreamed of piloting the Concorde, never got a chance
Would have been an American astronaut
Similar to: Yves Rossy (Swiss rocketman)

Angela Dicter

Private Detective, Mercedes-Benz, Stuttgart
Age 48
Has made career of researching bogus Mercedes-Benz parts
Member of Interpol's global network
Shapely; gymnast in college
Fluent in five languages
Similar to: Morena Baccarin ("V" actress)

John Baldinger

Patent Attorney based in Washington, DC
Age 55
6 feet tall, 185 pounds, dark features, mustache, horn-rim reading glasses
Similar to: Liam Neeson

Orin Wright

FAA Administrator, 35 years in U.S. Government service
Age 60
Astronaut service applicant (not selected)
Private pilot, instrument rated
Flies twin-engine Cessna at Frederick, Maryland, airport
Similar to: Neil Armstrong

Paula Frankel

FAA analyst, electrical engineer, subject matter expert
Age 41
Former astronaut applicant; electrical engineer
5 foot 6, slight but busty, long black hair
Very incisive, focused, driven, at times sharp tongued
Similar to: Sally Ride

Peter Wong

Senior Detective, Hong Kong Police Department
Age 50
Stocky, tenacious, nothing delicate about him. If he were a dog, he'd be a bulldog.
Trained at Scotland Yard in London
Cracked several smuggling rings in Hong Kong
Similar to: Chinese version of Columbo

Winston Barrister

Detective, Hong Kong Police Department
Age 52
Reports to Wong; Chinese mother
Graduated from Oxford with honors
Trains police in offensive and defensive driving.
Looks "British gentleman"
Similar to: Lord Mountbatten

Jennings Werner

First Independent U.S. President
Age 50
New Englander
Tall, imposing, large hands for shaking "politicking"
Successful lawyer turned legislator
Master of backroom deals
Similar to: Reminds one of a large John F. Kennedy

Rita Morales

President's appointment secretary, aide
Age 44 (looks 34)
Tall, delicate Spanish features
Raised in Miami, longtime friend of José Diaz
Comes across as an efficiency expert
Water sports hobbyist
Similar to: TV's Natalie Morales

Jefferson Palmer

U.S. Secretary of Defense
Age 53
University of Virginia graduate; retired USAF two-star general
Tall black man; Thunderbird pilot
Focused leader, talks in five-word sentences
Similar to: Colin Powell

Adam Aurum

U.S. Secretary of the Treasury
Age 60
Former Princeton economics professor
Famous for his financial and fiscal reasoning
Considered for Federal Reserve governorship
Similar to: TV commentator Eric Sevareid

Reid Burnham

CIA director, cybersecurity expert
Age 52
Long career with FBI, DHS
Princeton grad; majored in computer science
Friend of President Werner
Medium build, light, almost pale
Looks through you with penetrating eyes
Similar to: Tommy Lee Jones

Bill Cavanaugh

President's campaign manager
Age 46
Soured on Welfare State (Democrats), converted to Independent to run Werner's machine
Born and bred in Dallas, Texas
Southern accent
Avid balloonist and bird photographer
Simple slogans for complex ideas
Similar to: Douglas MacArthur

Clayton Feller

President's chief economist
Age 62
Works will with Adam Aurum
Nobel Prize laureate on job creation
Former director of the Cato Institute
Similar to: Warren Buffett

Tyrone Dobbs

NFL commissioner
Age 49
Lawyer, former president of the Players Union
Large black man
Similar to: Michael Strahan

Cheryl Clark

Member of Rose Bowl Commission
Age 45
Black, MBA from UCLA, knows every type of rose
Concert promoter/organizer/fund-raiser
Slender, tall, delicate features, graceful
Very effective speaker, women's advocate
Similar to: Halle Berry

Harvey Rubinstein

Former NYPD Police Commissioner
Age 54
Internationally known security expert
Helicopter pilot in Marine Corps
Moved to California to be near family
Short, powerful physique
Similar to: TV crime solver John Walsh

CPSIA information can be obtained at www.ICGtesting.com
Printed in the USA
BVOW05s0330080515

399490BV00001B/43/P